"The baby is my responsibility."

Lana's heart sank. If that's all the baby meant to Blake, then she'd better disabuse him of his overworked sense of obligation right away. "It's mine, too. This baby has two parents—two people who didn't think about the consequences of their actions."

Lana blushed, remembering how right it had felt to be in Blake's arms. How could something that felt so right be wrong? "It was irresponsible of both of us, but I don't regret it," she said softly. "Something very special came of our union."

"I always live up to my obligations. And the baby needs a father. We'll be married just as soon as I can arrange it."

"What if I say no?"

Dear Reader,

The forecast this spring is for SHOWERS! Not the gloomy, wet kind that bring May flowers, but the baby, bachelor and wedding kind that brings happiness and true love.

And you're invited to all three! This month, Pam McCutcheon hosts a baby shower for our heroine who's struck by an unexpected heat wave when in walks a surprise guest—the sexy *secret* daddy!

Then join us the next two months for an unusual bachelor party in Karen Toller Whittenburg's *A Bachelor Falls*, and for a raucous bridal shower in Debbi Rawlins's *The Bride To Be...or Not To Be?*

Confetti's falling this spring at American Romance! Don't miss out on any of the fun!

Happy reading!

Sincerely,

Debra Matteucci
Senior Editor & Editorial Coordinator
Harlequin
300 E. 42nd St.
New York, NY 10017

Here Comes The...Baby

PAM McCUTCHEON

Harlequin Books

TORONTO • NEW YORK • LONDON
AMSTERDAM • PARIS • SYDNEY • HAMBURG
STOCKHOLM • ATHENS • TOKYO • MILAN
MADRID • WARSAW • BUDAPEST • AUCKLAND

Thanks to Deb, Paula, Carol, Laura, Karen and Von for always being there when I need help. Special thanks to Rick Watson for his plotting assistance and to Linda Andraschko for being so generous as to read and critique the whole manuscript.
My gratitude also goes to Karen Toller Whittenburg and Debbi Rawlins for making my first series experience a fun one, and most especially to Denise O'Sullivan— for believing in me.

ISBN 0-373-16722-9

HERE COMES THE...BABY

Copyright © 1998 by Pamela S. McCutcheon

Chapter One

Lightning flashed outside the Salt Lake City-bound jet, illuminating sheets of driving rain as if they were silver needles against the dark velvet sky. Blake Warner rescued his drink as the storm-tossed plane rocked in another gust of wind. He doubted the flight attendants would be able to get him another one—everyone was buckled in their seats.

Blake had planned to work during the flight but the weather made that impossible. Searching for something to do, he glanced at the woman in the window seat next to him. Accustomed to sharing first class with suited businessmen and women or the occasional vacationing executive's family, Blake was hard put to categorize her. She appeared to be traveling alone, and she wasn't dressed like any businesswoman he knew.

Her soft, flowing dress revealed a body full of curves beneath the tiny lavender-flowered print and delicate lace collar. And instead of being tamed into submission, her dark blond hair cascaded in soft waves down her back, framing a graceful neck.

She was the most *feminine* woman he'd ever seen. And the saddest. The tears streaming down her cheeks rivaled the rain outside, though, surprisingly, they didn't mar the perfection of her face. As he watched, she sniffed and dabbed at her eyes with a shredded tissue.

Blake sighed. He hated getting involved in other people's problems, but even more, he hated having nothing to do. Coming to a sudden decision, he said, "I see we have showers inside as well as outside." He smiled to take the edge off his words.

She looked at him in bewilderment, her big brown eyes wet with tears. "What?"

He pointed to the window. "The rain." At her blank look, he said, "Never mind," and took out his handkerchief. "Here."

Lightning illuminated her halfhearted smile as she accepted the piece of cloth, fingering the fine material. "Thank you. I—I ran out of tissues."

He grinned. "It's all right. I always keep one on hand for damsels in distress." Blake didn't know what prompted him to tease her. She wasn't his usual type, but something in her forlorn manner pulled at him, making him want to act like a white knight.

Her smile widened a bit and she bobbed her head. "Thank you, kind sir. Do you run into damsels in distress often?"

"No," he admitted. "You're the first. I don't see them much in my line of work."

"And what's that?"

Glad to see his distraction was working, Blake said, "Construction. My company specializes in resorts and hotels. What do you do?"

"I teach school," she said, and dabbed at her nose.

"Really? You don't look like a schoolteacher."

She *was* soft and womanly though—the type of teacher he would have liked as a child.

She glanced at him in surprise. "What do teachers look like?"

"Well, mine were all ancient and decrepit."

She smiled and wiped a tear away. "I think it's just a matter of perspective—my students think *I'm* old and decrepit. I teach first through third grade."

"All three?"

"Yes, it's a small town."

A small-town schoolteacher? Once more he wondered what she was doing in first class. "What town is that?"

"Oh, you've probably never heard of it. Bachelor Falls, Missouri." Her eyes turned soft and dreamy. "It's the most beautiful place in the world."

Fishing, he said, "Just the place to raise a family?" She didn't wear a ring, but you never knew.

"Not anymore," she choked out. Tears welled up in her eyes once more and he cursed himself for causing the waterworks to start again.

Not knowing what to say or do, he just stared at the seat in front of him.

"I—I'm sorry," she said. "I don't mean to be so weepy."

"It's okay."

Her knowing expression called him a liar and Blake felt a little guilty. Okay, so he'd lied, but he doubted she wanted to hear the truth—that he'd rather be staked out naked on an anthill than listen to a woman cry.

Unlike the movies, where tears seemed to make men want to gratify a woman's every wish, all they did was frustrate Blake. In his experience, weeping women didn't want his help or wisdom—they just wanted comfort. Though he failed to see what good it would do, he still felt compelled to offer it.

"Would you like to talk about it?" he asked.

She cast him a rueful look. "You don't want to hear my problems."

"You're right, I don't."

She glanced at him in surprise.

Good—a little shock therapy might help. He added gently, "But I'd rather hear you talk than cry."

She fumbled with her seat belt. "I'll just go—"

"Don't be silly." He halted her attempt to stand up. "It's dangerous. Besides, the flight's full. There's nowhere else to sit."

She wiped her nose. "You're right, I forgot. I got the last seat on the plane." She glanced at him hesitantly, as if wondering if he would be a good confidant or not.

"Why don't we talk about something else," he suggested. "Like, your name?"

"Lana Talbot."

That was better—she was starting to dry up. "And I'm Blake Warner. So, tell me about Bachelor Falls."

"It's near Branson. Have you heard of it?"

"I think so. Doesn't it have something to do with music?"

"Yes, country-western music."

Over the next hour, they chatted about life in her small town and the people who lived there. They had to lean in close to hear each other over the noise of the storm, and the dimmed lights and comforting enclosure of their leather seats made an intimate shelter for two.

It felt as if they were isolated from the rest of the

world. It was an odd sensation, and Blake wondered at himself. He'd avoided letting anyone get close for years, yet this small-town schoolteacher made him feel like a child again, whispering shared secrets with his best friend beneath the bedcovers while the storm raged outside.

After one particularly large bump, an announcement came over the speakers. The airline regretted the inconvenience, but the severity of the storm required them to divert to Las Vegas. Connecting flights wouldn't be available until late the following morning.

Blake frowned. It was a pain, but he could postpone tomorrow's meeting. Besides, he had most of his work with him and could work at the hotel.

"Oh, no," Lana said.

"What's wrong?"

"I spent most of my money to get the last seat on this plane so I could get home. I don't have enough left for a hotel. What am I going to do?"

"Don't worry," Blake said. "They'll put us up somewhere."

Unfortunately, he was wrong. Once inside the terminal amid the clang and clamor of the slot machines, they learned the airline didn't consider themselves responsible for the bad weather. All they could do was apologize and offer round-trip transportation to the hotel of their choice.

Lana's stricken gaze tugged at Blake. After all, he was the one who'd told her it was going to be all right. He had to make it up to her to keep his armor from tarnishing.

"I'll loan you some money," he offered.

"Oh, no, I couldn't."

They argued about it for a few minutes, but small-town mores wouldn't let her accept money from a stranger and she was reluctant to call home and ask her family.

She looked worn-out, exhausted from weeping and worrying. Wondering what had landed her in this predicament, Blake said, "Well, you have to get some sleep."

She glanced around at the terminal. "Do you think they'll let me sleep here?"

"How can you?" he yelled over the incessant noise of the slot machines. "The din is unbearable. Tell you what, why don't you come with me? You can sack out while I finish the work I wasn't able to get to on the plane." She needed a good night's sleep and she wouldn't get it here.

Though she gave him a dubious glance, he could see she was tempted. "I don't know. I hate to disturb you."

Oddly, she seemed to trust him, and that warmed a small place in his heart. "You won't bother me," he promised. "I always get a suite anyway, so you can sleep in the bedroom while I work in the living room."

"But I don't want to take your bed," she protested.

"Okay, then," he teased her. "When I'm ready to go to sleep, I'll just dump you on the floor."

At her tentative smile, he added, "They usually have a couch in the other room that makes into a bed. I'll use it. It won't be an inconvenience, honest."

She still looked doubtful, so he added, "I couldn't sleep knowing my damsel was wandering the airport, begging for handouts. What kind of white knight would I be if I left you to the mercies of one-armed bandits and glassy-eyed gamblers?''

Her smile widened. "In that case, I accept. I'd hate to trouble my white knight."

"Good. It's settled then."

As they found transportation and made their way to a nearby hotel, Blake wondered why he had taken such an interest in this woman. With his many relatives pushing and pulling at him all the time, he hated taking on additional responsibility. So...Why? He didn't know, except that he felt they'd formed a close friendship on the plane. And he couldn't let a friend down.

After they entered the hotel suite and shook the water from their rain-soaked coats, Blake swung his briefcase up on the table. It was almost ten o'clock, still early enough to get some work done.

"Can I use the phone?" Lana asked. "I need to call my family."

"Of course." Blake hung up his garment bag and tried not to listen to Lana's conversation, but it was impossible not to overhear.

"Aunt Ona Mae? Is Mom there? I'm sorry, I know it's late, but—" A pause, then, "No, don't wake her. Sorry, we have a bad connection." Then, louder, she repeated, "It's the storm—a bad connection...no, I'm in Las Vegas."

There was an odd little catch in her voice, then she said, "Johnny's married. Where? I don't know—he's gone back to his air force base, I guess. I'll be home tomorrow. *Tomorrow.* Tell Mom, okay?" Then in a forceful tone, she said, "But don't tell anyone else."

She hung up and faced Blake with a rueful smile. "Sorry, we had a bad connection."

He gestured helplessly. "I couldn't help but over-hear."

Her mouth twisted in a grimace. "Then you know my fiancé dumped me for another woman."

"Dumped you?"

"Yes—it's still hard to believe. We were engaged for two years while he was stationed in Japan. He didn't want to get married until he was discharged from the air force, so I flew to California to visit him for Thanksgiving...and to try to convince him to change his mind. Some holiday."

She slumped down on the bed and rubbed a hand across her face. "He changed his mind, all right. The creep married someone else."

"Why didn't he tell you before?"

"Because he's a coward. He's afraid Bachelor Falls would turn against him for marrying an Asian woman, so he didn't tell anyone."

What a sorry excuse for a man. "Not even his family?"

"No, his parents died a few years ago, and he doesn't have any close relatives living. He has friends in Bachelor Falls though, so he still considers it home."

"So he used you to make himself look good."

"Unfortunately, yes. But after the way I chewed him out, I bet his ears are still ringing."

"Good for you." No wonder she was so upset. Blake shook his head in amazement. How could anyone dump Lana? She was the most *womanly* woman he'd ever met. "You're better off without him."

Uh-oh. That was the wrong thing to say. She turned away and he could see her shoulders shaking. He sat down on the bed, laying a tentative hand on her arm. "I'm sorry, I didn't mean to make you cry."

She turned into his shoulder and sobbed as if her heart would break, burrowing into him as if he were her only solace in the world.

Feeling awkward, he held her, trying to impart some comfort. How did he get himself involved in these situations? Especially when he so assiduously tried to avoid them. Blake told himself not to get involved. He'd had enough responsibilities thrust on him by his family. He didn't need any more.

Finally, her tears dried up and she pulled away from him, only to settle herself more comfortably in his lap. Caught off guard by her trusting head on his shoulder, he whispered, "Do you want to talk about it now?"

She hesitated, so he added, "I think you need to get it off your chest." He grinned. "Consider it part of the white knight service."

She smiled and cuddled close. "It's just that Johnny and I have been sweethearts since first grade. I had so many plans...." She continued, speaking of her longing for a home and a family as Blake rocked her like a child.

She eventually wound down, and he realized he ought to release her, and send her off to sleep. But her feminine curves and sweet-scented hair soon brought decidedly unchivalrous thoughts, not to mention the inevitable male reaction.

He shifted in discomfort, bringing her soft bottom even more in contact with his hardness. He stifled a groan and she stared at him in surprise, lifting slightly off his lap.

Embarrassed he released his hold on her. "I'm

sorry, I—'' He broke off, not knowing how to apologize.

"It's okay," she said, and melted back into his arms. "I'm flattered."

"Flattered?" Of all the responses she could have made, that was the last one he'd expected.

She smiled at him from beneath her lashes and put her arms around his neck. "Yes, it's nice to know *someone* still wants me." She gazed at him with an earnest, almost wistful expression. "Would you like to kiss me, Blake?"

Would he! A man could drown himself in her sensual beauty. "I don't want to take advantage of you. You're vulnerable right now—"

She stopped his lips with her kiss and Blake couldn't help but give in. His heart leapt like a wild thing as he slanted his mouth across hers and drank of her greedily. His hands found the lush mound of her breast and the sweet curve of her bottom beneath her filmy dress. He caressed them both, winning moans from her lips.

She kissed him with deep, plunging strokes of her tongue, running her hands through his hair and gliding them over his back and chest, immersing both of them in a total sensory experience. Blake had never met a woman so sensual. She fascinated him, drugging him with the depth of her need and desire. He wanted nothing more than to lose himself in her, but he drew back. This wasn't right.

She stared up at him with kiss-swollen lips, her hair tumbling in sexy profusion about her shoulders. Then with a slow, seductive movement, she drew him back into her embrace. "Love me, Blake," she whispered.

And, Lord help him, he did.

LANA WOKE, feeling disoriented and wondering why her surroundings looked so unfamiliar. When her gaze fell on the dark head of the man lying next to her, it all came flooding back—Johnny's marriage, the flight, Blake's rescue…and making love to a total stranger.

She buried her face in the pillow and moaned. What an idiot she'd been. Johnny's betrayal had hurt so much that she'd thrown herself at the first man she'd met.

Luckily Blake had been very sweet. Not to mention attractive. She raised her head to glance at him. He was sprawled in sleep, the twisted sheet around his hips white against his tanned skin…skin that covered a body to die for. Though his eyes were closed, she remembered how his blue gaze had flared with passion as his clever hands discovered the secret places of her body.

Lana felt her face warm in embarrassment. He'd had no choice—she'd attacked him last night like a sex-crazed nympho. That wasn't her usual style, but she'd been so upset that she'd needed comfort…and Blake had such comforting arms. Her white knight had been so kind, so nice and so downright sexy that she'd brazenly seduced him.

Her face grew even warmer as she realized she'd treated him as her own private plaything—a sex toy. Not exactly proper damsel behavior. Mortified, she wondered what he would think of her.

It didn't matter. She yearned to slip back into his embrace, to stroke that hard body, feel the silky texture of his hair, but there was no way she could face him this morning.

She slipped out of bed and dressed as fast and quietly as she could, then caught a ride to the airport and left on the first plane headed toward home. Once on the plane, she relaxed, knowing she'd never see him again.

THE PEAL OF THE DOORBELL woke Lana from a deep sleep. She opened bleary eyes, glad to note that this time, her surroundings were familiar. She checked the bedside clock, unsurprised to see it was morning. After getting home late yesterday afternoon, she'd crashed, exhausted by travel and emotion.

The bell rang again, then she heard the door open and her mother call out a cheery hello. Lana groaned. At times like this, she wished she'd never given her mother a key. She was in no mood to answer anyone's questions about Johnny and what he'd done to her. Thank heavens no one ever had to find out about Blake.

Reluctantly, she dragged herself out of her soft, warm bed, pushed the hair out of her eyes and pulled on a robe. Her mother met her at the bedroom door.

"There you are." Serena Talbot engulfed Lana in a big hug. "I'm so happy for you. But why couldn't you wait a little longer? You know your friends wanted to give you a big shower." She released Lana and grabbed her hand to drag her down the hall. "Not like that poor excuse for a shower Melva Whiffington's daughter had last month. I declare..."

Shower? Lana tried to clear her sleep-fogged brain and make sense of what her mother was saying. When they reached the kitchen, Serena waved her daughter into a chair and, still chattering, moved to the coffeepot.

From long practice, Lana waited for a pause, then dived in. "Wait, Mom. What are you talking about?"

Her mother froze in the act of scooping coffee grounds and gave her a surprised look. "Your wedding shower, dear."

Something was wrong here. "But Johnny and I aren't getting married. Didn't Aunt Ona Mae tell you?"

"Well, of course. You're already married."

"No—Johnny is, but I'm not. He married someone else."

Serena plopped down in the chair and stared at her daughter, her mouth agape. "Someone else? Who?"

"It doesn't matter—just some woman he met overseas."

"But why?"

"He said he fell in love with her."

"But...he's been in love with you for years."

Lana's mouth twisted in a grimace. "Apparently not. He was only in like with me...or so he said. But he was too much of a coward to tell me on the phone and you know he never writes, so he waited until I got there to tell me." Waited until she'd flown hundreds of miles to destroy her hopes and dreams.

"Oh, honey. I'm so sorry."

She shrugged, wondering why she wasn't more upset. Probably because she'd cried herself out on the plane. To tell the truth, her pride was hurt more than anything else, and she began to wonder if she'd really loved Johnny as much as she'd thought. "What did Auntie Om tell you?"

"She said you and Johnny got married in Las Vegas because he had to go back to his base overseas."

Lana groaned. It was just like Aunt Ona Mae to

mess things up! "No. Good grief, why would you believe that?"

"Well, you were engaged. And why else would you be calling from Las Vegas?"

"Because the storm grounded my plane there." Trying to block out the memory of what she'd done in Las Vegas, Lana changed the subject. "Why was Auntie at your house anyway?" If her mother had answered the phone, this mix-up wouldn't have happened.

Her mother waved her hand vaguely. "Oh, she had a dream that the aliens put up invisible cameras in her bedroom."

Dear Aunt Ona Mae—she saw alien conspiracies under every bush. Conveniently, sometimes. She must have been lonely that night. "Cameras, huh?" Lana said. "Well, I see why you'd have to let her sleep over."

Aunt Ona Mae had thought out her delusion very well. She insisted the aliens came from a planet called Bost and they planned to abduct her as they had her fiancé so many years ago. But she'd been foiling their dastardly plans for years by following the instructions in her dreams.

Sure, Auntie Om was dotty and always poking her nose into everyone else's business, but she meant well. Lana and her mother shared an amused smile, until her mother's turned to a look of consternation.

"What's wrong?"

"Oh, dear. Ona Mae."

Realization struck. "She didn't," Lana said in rising horror. "I told her not to tell anyone but you."

"You know she can't keep a secret."

"You mean..." Apprehension filled her. Did she want to hear this?

Her mother laid a consoling hand on Lana's and nodded. "It's all over town that you and Johnny got married in Las Vegas."

Lana groaned and buried her face in her hands. She should have known. With twenty-four hours and a hot secret in her possession, Aunt Ona Mae would have told everyone in town by now. Of course, she would have sworn them all to secrecy first—she did have her ethics.

"So now everyone thinks I'm married to Johnny." Lana sighed and raised her head. That made it even worse. "Well, we'll just have to tell them the truth."

"No, you can't do that," her mother protested, a stricken look on her face. When she got flustered, Serena couldn't keep her hands still, and they fluttered madly now. She rushed on. "Let them think you're married. After all, he's overseas. No one will know."

She couldn't do that. "But, Mom—"

"You said yourself Johnny never writes. He never calls either, so who's to know?"

"Mom, stop. Think about what you're saying. What's wrong with you?"

The stricken look deepened. "I—I told Melva you were married."

"Mother, did you have to?" Silly question. Of course she had to. Melva Whiffington was her mother's arch rival. They'd competed for everything since they were children—men when they were younger, now flower shows and pie-baking contests and, of course, their daughters' achievements. "Well, you'll just have to tell her the truth."

"I can't eat my words. Not with *Melva.*"

"You never should have told her in the first place."

Serena dropped her gaze. "I know, but she was so superior when her daughter got married last month. I *had* to tell her."

Lana sighed in resignation. "Yes, I see that, but I don't want to live a lie. You'll have to tell her the truth."

Her mother clasped Lana's hand with a pleading look. "Please, can't we keep it a secret for a little while? Just until I can figure out a way to explain it?"

Maybe it wouldn't be so wrong to postpone the pain a little, until she was more ready to deal with it. "How long?"

"Two months?"

"Mom!"

"Okay, one month. Please?"

Lana shook her head. Sometimes she felt like the parent instead of the child. But what would it hurt? She'd give Mom a month, then tell the truth. "All right. But I need to tell my best friends." She'd never kept anything from Ellie Applegate and Kelly St. James.

"No," her mother pleaded. "They don't need to know. Please? Just for a little while."

"But if I don't, they'll want to give me a shower. I don't want that—it wouldn't feel right."

"No shower, I promise. I'll tell them you want to wait for Johnny." Serena stared at her daughter with a pleading expression.

Defeated, Lana sighed. "Okay. I won't tell anybody for one month, but that's it."

THREE WEEKS LATER, Lana had cause to regret that agreement many times over. She sat on her bed, clutching her favorite stuffed animal, reluctant to venture out. She'd lost track of the number of times people had asked her about her wedding or about her missing wedding band or when Johnny was coming home.

She'd tried to brush them off, pretending she was too upset about Johnny being overseas. But putting them off just made things worse. When people didn't have the facts, they made things up—especially in Bachelor Falls.

The last Lana had heard, she'd been married by Elvis with Wayne Newton and Dolly Parton in attendance. Poor Johnny hadn't had time to buy her a ring because he had to hurry through the ceremony so he could fly back to Japan to single-handedly quell a native uprising.

She was still shaking her head at that last one. But that wasn't the worst of it. The worst part was that she'd had to put Ellie and Kelly off with so many excuses they were beginning to get upset with her. Grateful the month was almost up, Lana dreaded to think what would happen when they learned the truth. She'd tell them right after Christmas, even if it would put a damper on the holiday season. She was sick and tired of evasions.

And now she'd find out if her latest worry had any basis in fact. She hugged Purple Bunny tighter, delaying the moment of truth. The stuffed animal was worn and ragged, with one ear hanging limply over a missing eye, but she loved him just the same. Believing he brought good luck, she and her two best friends had traded him back and forth throughout childhood on special occasions. They'd added and removed stickers and buttons to his plush body as the whim took them, and secreted mysterious notes in the zipper compartment intended for a little girl's pajamas.

The notes were only taken out when one of them needed an answer to an important question. Surprisingly, the answer was usually helpful, so they'd continued the tradition on into adulthood. And now, even though they were approaching thirty, they still passed him around like a giant purple fortune cookie.

Now it was Lana's turn to have him. She stroked his good ear and whispered into it. "What will be the outcome of this test?"

She unzipped the pouch and removed the note. *Though times are difficult now, things will improve and, in the end, you will be happier than ever before.*

She let out the breath she didn't know she'd been holding. It wasn't an answer to her immediate question, but she hoped it was true anyway. Lana glanced at the test stick lying innocently on the bathroom sink. There was the real answer. But, what did she want the answer to be? Well, time was up and she had to know. Sighing, she put Purple Bunny down and picked up the stick.

She knew it. She was pregnant.

Her front door opened and Lana heard her mother call out, "Yoo-hoo."

"In here, Mom," Lana said, feeling numb.

Her mother breezed in to the bedroom and stopped when she saw the stick in her daughter's hand. "Is that what I think it is?"

Lana nodded, trying to push back the jumble of emotions roiling through her.

"Are you...?"

She nodded again. "I'm going to have a baby."

"Oh, honey." Her mother folded her in her comforting arms. "How could Johnny do this to you?"

"It—it wasn't Johnny."

Her mother pulled away, looking shocked. "Then who?"

She avoided her mother's gaze, but she'd never kept anything from her before and wasn't going to start now. "A—a man I met. In Las Vegas."

"A stranger?" her mother exclaimed. It sounded even worse when someone else said it. "That's not like you."

"I know." How could she make her mother understand that she'd fallen hard for a man's kindness and sense of humor, that she'd needed to feel connected to the world somehow? That she'd casually used his body and tossed him aside?

How could she when she didn't understand it herself? "I...needed comfort," she explained.

"Can you find him again?"

"I don't know but I guess I'd better try."

"Do you know his name?"

"Jeez, Mom. Of course I know his name. But that's not important. What's important is that I'm going to have a baby...without a father." Even if she could find Blake, she couldn't imagine him wanting to marry her on the basis of a one-night stand. And she wasn't sure she wanted him to anyway.

"Oh, honey." Serena enveloped her in another hug, and Lana thanked heaven her mother didn't ask the other question.

Her entire life, all Lana had wanted was to have a loving husband, lots of children and a happy home.

She wanted a marriage just like her parents had enjoyed before her father died—loving and giving.

Spreading her hand over the spot where a new life was growing inside her, Lana knew that, husband or no, there was no way she was going to get rid of this baby or let anyone else raise it. It was all hers. "I'm keeping it," she said simply.

Her mother's expression softened. "I know. You couldn't do anything else." Serena patted her hand. "We'll just tell everyone that Johnny's dead."

"Mother! We can't do that."

"Why not?"

"Well, for one thing, he's *not* dead. And he may not write or phone much, but he's bound to show up sooner or later."

"Then we'll just have to find you another husband."

Lana frowned. Not just any man would do. She wanted someone she could love, like sweet, crazy Johnny. She amended that thought. Irresponsible Johnny was more like it. "Like who?"

Her mother stood, then started pacing. "Who didn't shower last year?"

To anyone outside Bachelor Falls, this might have sounded like an overly personal question, but any resident would know Serena was talking about the local legend. It had originated sometime in the 1800s and stated that to remain single, every unmarried man in town over the age of eighteen had to shower in the nearby falls before sundown on Falls Day during Bachelor Daze. If they didn't, they were fated to marry within the year.

The town believed fervently in the legend, and the annual Bachelor Daze festival had become a frantic competition as the married men helped the bachelors and the women tried to keep them from reaching the falls before sundown. That's why Johnny had been such a good candidate. His assignment overseas had made him miss the last festival.

Well, the legend had worked once more. Only this time, the bachelor had married the wrong woman. But, to be honest, there *was* another candidate. "The only one who didn't shower last year and isn't engaged already is Ned Laney."

Serena's face brightened. "Perfect! Ned's adored you for years. I'm sure he'll marry you."

"But I don't want to marry him." He was a good friend but he just didn't ring her chimes.

"Why not? He's nice, good-looking, he has a good job and he's great with kids."

"Yes, but I want more than that in a marriage." Lana gazed at her mother with an earnest expression. "I want what you and Dad had."

Serena gave her a compassionate look. "I want that for you, too, but love like that is very rare. Do you want your child growing up without a father?"

"Better that than a loveless childhood. Besides, this baby already has a father."

"Are you sure you can find him?" Serena asked, hope evident in her voice.

"It shouldn't be too difficult." He probably lived in California or Salt Lake City, since that's where the plane had been headed. How hard could it be to hunt him down?

"How do you think he'll react?"

"I have no idea but I have to find him."

Her mother gave her a doubtful look. "That might take a while. What are we going to tell people in the meantime? They're bound to find out as soon as you go to Dr. Evans.''

True—Dr. Evans's nurse was an inveterate gossip. Much as Lana hated the thought of it, she said, ''Why don't we tell them the truth?''

''Don't be silly. Imagine what Melva would say. We can't do that. At least, not until we find you a husband.''

Lana shook her head. All would be forgiven if she only had a man? Sometimes she wondered about people. But right now she was too confused to discuss it. She needed to think—think about what would be best for the future and her baby.

Her mother grabbed her shoulders. ''Promise me,'' she demanded. ''Promise me you won't tell anyone about this until we find you a husband.''

''I think they'll figure it out in few months when I start to show.''

''I mean Johnny. Promise me you won't tell them about Johnny. Let them think the baby is his.''

Lana shrugged, not caring at the moment. ''Okay, for now.'' She stood and faced her mother with a stern expression. ''But the most important thing is my baby. I won't let anyone hurt it. Especially not anyone's small-minded attitude. If I have to, I'll move away.''

''Okay, okay,'' her mother said swiftly. ''But that won't be necessary. You'll see.''

Lana tightened her lips. ''Maybe.'' She was going to make sure her baby had the best possible life, no matter what she had to do. Nothing was more important. Nothing.

Chapter Two

The sun was setting over the Dallas skyline when Blake's office door opened and Grace Warner stuck her head inside. "Your mother called again," she said.

"Mother?" Blake searched his mind, trying to figure out what chore he'd forgotten, but couldn't think of anything. "What did she want?"

"She didn't say."

He rubbed a hand over his face. Knowing his mother, it was probably some new task she'd dreamed up, like counseling one of his young cousins about the bad company they kept or bailing an uncle out of trouble. If it wasn't one thing, it was another.

"Don't worry," Grace said with a smile. "I lied for you. I told her you'd gone for the day."

"Thanks. Remind me to give you a raise."

She deserved one. Invaluable when it came to keeping him organized and remembering all the details of the construction company, Grace was the perfect assistant. She'd make an even better vice president, just as soon as Blake's father agreed to the promotion.

Like all the Warners, she'd started at the bottom.

Unlike his other cousins, she'd made herself so indispensable that he'd promoted her to his personal assistant five years ago. He hadn't regretted it either. She probably knew the company better than he did. She certainly enjoyed it more.

"She's worried about you," Grace said.

"I know." But that didn't stop his mother from depending on him, just like everyone else in the family.

Grace came in and sat in front of his desk, giving him a look that challenged him to blow her off. "What's wrong?"

"Wrong?"

"Don't give me that." The command should have sounded odd coming from her diminutive frame, but Grace didn't mince words with anyone. "You've changed. Ever since you got stranded in Las Vegas, you've been different."

"Different how?" Blake hedged. Had his preoccupation with Lana Talbot become evident?

"You know. For almost four months now, you've been working longer hours, never giving yourself any free time, never going out."

Blake shrugged. "I like to keep busy."

"Bull," Grace said. "What happened?"

That was what came of making a co-worker out of someone who'd known him since he was a smart-aleck teenager. Grace never cut him any slack. Knowing she would pester him until he told all, Blake said, "I met a woman in Las Vegas."

Grace's eyes brightened. "It's about time."

"No, it's not. I...can't get her out of my mind. I have to work or I do nothing but think about her."

Day and night. Especially night.

"That's wonderful."

"It's a pain." This had never happened before—he couldn't get anything done.

"Who is she? Someone I know?"

"No, she's not in the business at all."

"So," Grace urged, "tell me about her. And don't leave anything out." She crossed her legs and gazed at him with an expectant expression, obviously settling in for a long chat.

Maybe it would help purge him of Lana's memory. Lord knew nothing else had worked, and Grace was the perfect confidante—discreet, caring and nonjudgmental. He could trust her.

He sighed. "I met her on the plane. She was crying and didn't have enough money when the plane was grounded, so I offered to let her stay in my hotel room. One thing led to another and, well…"

Grace's knowing look said he didn't have to finish the sentence. "A one-night stand?"

He frowned. "No."

"So you've seen her since then?"

"No, I mean it didn't feel like a one-night stand." It had felt like home.

"Tell me about it," Grace whispered.

Knowing his thoughts and feelings were safe with her, Blake let his mind drift back to that night. "She was soft and womanly, and so…sensual I felt as if I was drowning in her. I started out giving her comfort, but she ended up giving it to me."

It had felt as if she'd possessed some strange power to encompass all of him with the lushness of her body, to make him feel as if nothing would ever be wrong again. He glanced up, embarrassed at revealing more than he'd intended.

Grace raised her eyebrows. "Wow. Sounds like quite a woman. But...not your usual type."

"I know." He usually preferred sleek, sophisticated women who understood the game and how it was played—and never made any demands on him. It was safer that way. He didn't want any more needy dependents.

"Your mother will be thrilled."

He glared at her. "Don't you dare."

"Why not?" Grace's expression softened. "Don't you think she'll be glad to hear you're finally thinking seriously about someone?"

"She and Dad already have their favorite daughter-in-law candidates picked out. Besides, all it means to them is the opportunity for grandchildren. More Warners to take over the business and carry on the family name."

"That's part of it," Grace admitted. "But she's also concerned about you. She wants you to be happy."

It's too late. "Don't get her hopes up—it's not like I'm in a relationship. Heck, we don't even live in the same *state.*"

"Well, if it isn't a one-night stand and it isn't a relationship, what is it?"

A pain. "I don't know."

"Then there's one way to find out."

He gave her a dubious glance. "How?"

"Go see her."

"What?"

"You have to get her out of your system one way or another. See her again and find out why you're obsessing over her."

"What makes you think I'm obsessing?"

"Aren't you?"

Yes, but... "That's not the point."

"Isn't it? Now I know why you've been so surly the past few months—you haven't been getting any."

"Grace!" She was getting *way* too personal now.

"Don't think I haven't noticed you've stopped dating."

"Okay, maybe it's a little obsession."

"Then go see her."

"But the company—"

"Can get along without you for a week or two. Come on, Blake. We both know you've been moody. Heck, the whole company knows it. You need a break from us, and frankly, we need one from you, too." Her voice softened. "See if you can recapture the Blake we used to know."

"But I can't leave the Palladian Resort bid hanging."

She gave him a puzzled glance. "That's another thing you've been obsessing over. Why is that particular project so important?"

He toyed with a pen on his desk and kept his voice nonchalant. "Father doesn't want it known, but if I win this bid, he's promised to hand over controlling interest of the company."

"How'd you convince him to do that?"

"I threatened to quit altogether."

Grace's eyes widened. "You don't mean it."

"Yes, I do." He couldn't continue to butt heads with his father every day, and the company was suffering with two bosses.

She whistled. "Wow. You mean he's promised no more meddling, no more second-guessing, no more old-fashioned business methods?"

"You got it." And with his father out of the picture, Blake wouldn't have to worry so much about leaving the company for more than a few days. Hell, he might even be able to take a vacation.

"Finally!" She steepled her hands in supplication. "Then, please, win this bid."

"I plan to. That's why I can't afford to leave at this time."

Grace thought for a moment. "Yes, you could. The bid isn't due for a couple of months and you could work on some of it while you're gone. Besides, you're no good to us this way. You need to get this woman out of your system."

She was right. He could work on it from Missouri. And Lord knew he deserved a break—he hadn't taken a vacation in years. "Maybe I will."

"Good. Do it." She rose and headed for the door. "Oh, and when I said recapture the Blake we once knew, I didn't mean from four months ago—I'm talking about the happy-go-lucky, fun-loving Blake you used to be before you started working here."

Before he could answer that zinger, she swept out of the room. But if she thought he could be as he once was, she was mistaken. That Blake Warner was a lifetime ago. Even if he won the bid and gained control of the company, he still had too many people depending on him.

But Grace was right about one thing. Seeing Lana Talbot again was the only way to get her out of his system.

Two weeks later, his calendar clear, Blake headed for Bachelor Falls. He debated whether or not to tell Lana he was coming but decided not to. He hadn't admitted it to Grace, but that night in Las Vegas had assumed monumental proportions in his mind. But what if Lana had forgotten it? Or worse, what if she was angry at him for taking advantage of her vulnerability? He had to see her reaction firsthand and talk to her so he could judge for himself.

He rented a car at the Springfield airport and headed toward Bachelor Falls, enjoying the drive through the lush greenery and winding mountain roads. When he reached the town, he pulled into the lone motel, the Sky Hook, perched high on a hill.

Inside the lobby, there was no one but a middle-aged man behind the counter and a woman reading a tabloid in one of the orange plastic chairs.

Blake tried not to stare. She must be at least sixty, but she was dressed as if she were going to a fifties' sock hop, complete with a pink poodle skirt and a hair band holding her white hair in a stiff flip. Was she headed to a costume party, or was this the way she always dressed?

The man looked up and stared at Blake with interest. "Can I help you?"

"Yes. I'd like a room."

"Well, we got one," the man said and pulled out an ancient registration book.

Blake filled it out as the man poked his head into the room behind him and called out, "Esther, we have a guest."

A woman about the same age as the man came out and peered at Blake. The man said, "This here's Esther Williams and I'm Hank Williams." Hank stared at Blake, obviously looking for a reaction.

Unsure how he was supposed to respond, Blake said, "Really?"

It must have been what Hank was looking for. He hooted with laughter and slapped his leg. "Not them superstars, of course. Esther here's the singer and I'm the swimmer." He jerked a thumb at a yellowing photograph behind him.

In the picture, Esther wore a Western outfit and Hank's lanky, hairy form was encased in a woman's swimsuit and cap. But their whimsical attire was at odds with their *American Gothic* expressions. Strange people.

"See? We own the Sky Hook."

"I...see. Uh, nice to meet you."

As if that were some sort of cue, the poodle-skirted woman rose from her seat in the lobby and came over to check him out. He tried to ignore her, but found it difficult when she peered up his nostrils and palpated the area between his shoulder blades.

Startled, Blake pulled away, trying to get some distance from her prying fingers. "Can I help you?" he asked in a forbidding tone.

"This here's Ona Mae Hunyacre," Hank said.

Blake nodded at the odd woman and tried to keep his distance as he handed Hank his credit card.

"Blake Warner," Hank read aloud. "You're not from around here."

"That's right."

"Don't know any Warners. You have kin here?"

"No," Blake said, trying to discourage further questions.

It didn't work. Ona Mae's expression turned suspicious. "Where you from?" she barked.

"Uh, Dallas."

Her beady stare didn't waver. "Humph. Dallas, Texas, or Dallas...Bost?" she asked, scrutinizing his body as if she suspected he carried some alien parasite.

Bost? He glanced at Hank, but the old man didn't seem fazed by the question. "Texas, of course."

"Humph. That's what they all say."

She continued to glare at him as Hank asked, "Well, if you ain't got kin here, then why *are* you here?"

Hank didn't seem to understand how rude the question was, and the women's silent stares were a little unnerving. Searching for an excuse, Blake said, "I'm here on business."

"What kind of business you in?"

"I'm CEO of Warner Construction."

"Yeah? What do you build?"

"Lots of things, but we specialize in hotels and resorts." Changing the subject, he said, "Can I have my room key, please?" Anything to escape these oddballs.

Hank scratched his jaw. "Don't know why anyone would want to do any construction here."

"I'm not saying I am. I just heard about Bachelor Falls from one of your residents and thought I'd come take a look."

Hank brightened. "Oh? Who told you about us?"

Did these people never give up? Not wanting to appear too eager, Blake said, "Just a woman I met a few months ago. Said she was a schoolteacher. She has long blond hair and I think her name was…Lara?"

"That'd be Lana," Hank said.

"That's it." Right. As if he didn't remember every detail of their meeting. "Know where I can find her?" he asked in a casual tone.

"Why?" barked Ona Mae. "What you want with Lana?"

"I, uh, met her on the plane and she left something there. I'd like to...return it to her." She'd left something all right—lots of confusion.

The distrust on Ona Mae's face vanished and she patted his hand. "You must be the nice young man who helped her in Las Vegas."

That was a good sign. If Lana had spoken of him in positive terms, then maybe she wasn't angry with him. "That's me," he admitted weakly. "Do you, uh, know where I can find her?"

"She'll be at the party late this afternoon at the town hall," Ona Mae said, generous with information now that he'd apparently passed inspection. "After work."

"Party?" In the middle of the week?

"A baby shower," Hank explained. "You're welcome to come. Everyone will be there."

Blake wasn't crazy about the idea of attending a baby shower, but it sounded like the easiest and fastest way to meet Lana again. "Thanks. I'll do that."

Later that day, he followed Hank's directions to the town hall. Obviously the old building had been a theater at one time, sporting a stage at one end and lots of red velvet and gilt ornamentation. It was an interesting piece of Americana, but looked a little incongruous with the pink and blue shower decorations. Crepe paper and balloons festooned the hall, along with cardboard pictures of ducks and bunnies tacked up all over the walls.

The crowd didn't seem to find it unusual. Blake scanned the gathering for Lana but couldn't spot her. He did find Hank, who greeted him like a long-lost friend. Grabbing Blake's arm, Hank dragged him around to introduce him to people, telling everyone that Blake built resorts.

Mutterings and suspicious looks followed in their wake, but Blake ignored them. Instead, he continued to murmur polite greetings as he searched for Lana. Where was she?

A few minutes later, someone called out a warning and hushed the crowd, saying, "They're coming!"

"Good," Hank said with glee, and handed Blake a handful of cotton balls. "Here, you'll need these."

Blake took the soft things, wondering what the heck he was supposed to do with them.

Silence blanketed the room. There was Lana at last, standing between two other women. Blake's tension vanished. Damn, she looked even better than he'd remembered—beautiful and radiant.

"Surprise!" the crowd yelled. Those closest to the three women threw their cotton balls at them.

Lana looked shocked and pleased. Someone said, "Get up on stage now."

As the crowd called out good-natured welcomes, she and her two companions headed for the stage. The crowd parted for them, raining cotton balls all the way.

Since Blake was standing right in front of the stage, she was headed straight toward him. Before she reached him, Hank boomed out, "Well, Lana, since your husband couldn't be here for your baby shower, the whole dang town turned out."

Husband? Baby? Confused, Blake could do nothing but stare. Lana caught sight of him at that moment. Recognition dawned and her smile faded as the color drained from her face and her hand went to her throat. She gasped, then turned and bolted out the door.

Blake felt as shocked as she looked. Lana was married, pregnant and terrified of the sight of him.

Damn—just his luck.

ONCE OUTSIDE, Lana paused and gasped for breath. As her panic attack subsided, her thoughts darted in a hundred different directions and she spread her hand over the life growing inside her. She'd reacted instinctively to protect her baby, but now felt nothing but embarrassment. This sort of emotional reaction wasn't like her at all. How was she going to explain it? And what in the world was she going to do now?

"Honey, you all right?" her mother called out in worried tones.

Lana's best friends hurried out the door. Ellie closed the door behind her, saying, "Never mind, Mrs. T. We'll take care of her."

Despite her tight dress, Kelly reached Lana first and gave her a hug. "What's wrong? Are you sick?"

Ellie was a little slower, having given up her usual overalls and ball cap for a dress and heels in deference to the occasion. She grabbed Lana's arm and felt her forehead. "No, she's past that now. Remember, she said last week that the morning sickness had subsided. Besides, it's not morning."

"Yes, but some smells can make you sick when you're pregnant—no matter what time of day it is." Kelly squeezed Lana's shoulders. "Is that what it was?"

Lana shook her head numbly, trying to get her raging emotions under control. Fear and apprehension battled it out with growing pleasure. Blake must have come to find her. Why else would he be here in Bachelor Falls?

She'd tried for months to find him without success. Why did he have to show up now—just in time to hear her mother's lies? She pressed her fingers to her temples. Good Lord, what must he think of her? She had to set things straight.

Her friends exchanged worried glances at her continued silence and pulled her over to a nearby bench to sit down. "It was that man," Ellie said. "That stranger. She turned tail and ran when she saw him. Was that it?"

Lana nodded, wondering how she was going to explain.

Kelly patted her on the arm. "Good grief, why? I mean, he's got to be the best-looking guy I've seen around these parts in a lo-o-ong time."

She had that right. "I, uh, met him before." That was an understatement. *Met* was such an inadequate word to describe the passionate encounter they'd shared.

"What did he do to you?" Ellie demanded.

Nice things. *Very* nice things. "Nothing," Lana lied. "It just…startled me when I saw him again."

Her friends exchanged that look again. "Deer run when they're startled," Ellie said. "You don't. What's really wrong?"

Lana gestured helplessly. "I can't explain right now."

"Not even to us?" Kelly demanded.

"No, I promised." And she'd never regretted a promise more, but her mother was the only one who could release her from this one. Besides, she didn't have enough time to explain the whole mess.

"Shoot," Kelly said. "I knew we should have brought Purple Bunny to the shower."

Ellie rolled her eyes. "Don't be silly." Then to Lana, she said, "You want us to have the boys take him aside and ask him to leave?"

"No!" That was the last thing she wanted. This child was Blake's as much as it was hers and he had a right to know about it. "I...need to talk to him." She had no idea how he would react to the news, but he had to be told.

"Okay." Ellie glanced back toward the door. "But you're gonna have to go back in there, you know. Everyone is waiting."

"I know. Just give me a minute." Lana delayed the inevitable, not knowing what to do with the emotions whirling inside her. "It's hard enough dealing with the Pregnancy Police as it is."

Kelly chuckled. "The what?"

"Oh, you know, the well-meaning busybodies who say I can't lift this, can't eat that, or tell me about ridiculous superstitions I have to follow if I want a healthy baby. I call them the Pregnancy Police."

"Is it really that bad?" Kelly asked.

"Yes, but I could put up with them if it weren't for the Belly Buffers."

At her friends' raised eyebrows, Lana said, "The ones who come up and rub my stomach when they learn I'm pregnant. They don't even ask permission—it's like my belly has become public property." She smiled. "Now I know how little kids feel. I guess I should be glad they don't pinch my cheeks."

They laughed, and the door opened again. Ellie yelled out, "Just give her a minute—she's not feeling well." The door closed and Ellie patted Lana's hand.

"It's all right. We'll just tell the Pregnancy Police a smell made you sick."

Kelly grinned. "Yeah, tell 'em it was Mayor Bartlett's cigar. I've been trying to get that man to stop smoking those disgusting things anyway."

"That would be the truth," Lana said. "The smell makes me nauseous even when I'm not pregnant."

"Okay," Kelly said with relish. "I'll go tell him he has to get rid of it. You take your time and come in when you're ready."

When Kelly left, Lana turned to Ellie. "It didn't help that the shower caught me totally by surprise. I'm not quite five months' pregnant. Why are you giving me one now? I didn't expect it for another four months."

Ellie shrugged. "Well, everyone assumed you'll be moving to Japan to be with Johnny before you're too pregnant to travel."

Oh, yeah. She'd forgotten that rumor.

"Kelly and I wanted to give you one later, but the town was too antsy. After you eloped and didn't give us a chance to attend your wedding or give you a shower—"

"I didn't think it was right to have one without the groom here," Lana explained. Especially since there *was* no groom. She would have been mortified to accept gifts for a marriage that didn't exist. "I don't need anything anyway."

"Well, they figured since you deprived them of one shower, they were going to make up for it with this one." Ellie grinned. "You know how the town loves showers. And since it's April, it seemed so natural...."

"I know," Lana said with a sigh. How ironic they should choose April Fools' Day.

"You ready to go back inside now?"

"I guess." No sense postponing the inevitable any longer.

Kelly popped her head out the door. "It's okay," she called out. "The mayor put out his cigar and we opened some windows to get the smell out."

Reluctantly, Lana dragged herself to her feet and wondered how she looked. Bloated and white as a sheet, no doubt. Like a sick, pregnant lady.

She sighed. This wasn't how she'd envisioned telling Blake, but that would have to wait anyway. Providing, of course, that he stuck around long enough to hear it. She wouldn't blame him if he'd already taken off.

Lana let her friends lead her inside and she cast an uneasy glance at the crowd. They did mean well and had only her best interests at heart. She'd just pretend everything was wonderful.

"Sorry," she said around a strained smile. She sent the poor mayor an apologetic glimpse. He looked defiant, standing there with his unlit cigar clutched between his teeth.

She glanced around, noticing Blake was still there and watching her intently. Averting her gaze for fear she'd give herself away, she gave her mother a reassuring smile.

The rest of the shower was stressful, to say the least. With her friends standing beside her and discouraging anyone from getting close, Lana felt like a bone being fought over by a pack of dogs. And though she refused to meet Blake's eyes, she could feel his stare on her, feel his unanswered questions boring into her mind.

She somehow managed the appropriate oohs and ahs over the generous baby gifts, but was unable to enjoy them. Finally the time came when there were no more games to play, and no more gifts to open. She said her goodbyes and steeled herself to look at Blake, hoping he would understand the plea in her eyes.

Her mental telepathy must have worked, for he managed to make his way to where she was packing up. She straightened to meet him and said calmly, "Hello, Blake."

Ellie and Kelly came to stand guard again and he flicked a glance at them. "Can I talk to you alone?" he asked.

Ellie took a small step forward. "I don't think that's such a good idea."

Blake raised an eyebrow and gave her a charming smile, one that turned Lana's knees to mush. "I only want to talk."

It didn't work with Ellie. "She's not feeling well."

"Can you back off a little?" Lana asked gently. "Blake won't hurt me, and I would like to talk to him alone."

At least, she didn't think he'd hurt her. What did she know about him, anyway...other than the fact that he was an excellent lover and could charm the wood out of a woodchuck?

Kelly gave him an assessing glance. "All right, but we'll be close by if you need us. Within earshot," she said with emphasis.

Kelly and Ellie moved away, giving Blake warning glares. He smiled ruefully at Lana. "What do they think I'm going to do? Rip off your clothes and make mad, passionate love to you in front of this crowd?''

A girl could hope, couldn't she? She felt herself redden and his gaze raked her body with something resembling longing until it reached her stomach. Then his face turned stony, expressionless.

"Looks like someone already did that," he said. "Congratulations on your marriage."

"Things aren't exactly what they seem." Lana glanced at the people who were trying to eavesdrop on their conversation. This wasn't the place or the time to explain.

His mouth twisted in a grimace. "You mean you're not pregnant?"

"Well, yes, but—"

"And you're married. Look," he said, lowering his voice to a whisper only she could hear, "it might have been just a one-night stand to you but I thought..." He shrugged. "Never mind. It was just one of those things."

Her heart leapt with excitement. It had meant something to him, too. "No, it wasn't. I—I thought it was pretty special."

"So that's why you ran home and married the first man you met? Or did Johnny dump his wife for you?"

Stung, she had to acknowledge that's how it looked. But she couldn't explain with her friends moving closer, apparently drawn by the intensity of their conversation. "Please," she whispered, "it wasn't like that. Will you give me a chance to explain later, when we can be alone?"

He shrugged. "What's the point? You're married and expecting a baby. I...don't think we have much in common.'' He backed off and spoke louder. "I'll leave tomorrow and you'll never have to see me again.'' His mouth twisted in a parody of a smile. "Have a nice life.''

He turned abruptly and left. Lana wanted to cry out that she wasn't married, that she was carrying *his* baby, but she kept her mouth closed. She'd promised her mother she wouldn't create a scandal. Besides, she owed it to Blake to break this news to him in private.

As her solicitous friends hovered, Lana's mind spun with uncertainty. How could she keep Blake around long enough to talk to him alone and let him know he was the father of her child?

Chapter Three

Several people followed Lana home, insisting she couldn't carry anything in her condition. Wondering why they were never around when she needed help carrying in the groceries or mowing the lawn, Lana managed to shoo them out.

Unfortunately, her mother wouldn't be shooed. After everyone left, Serena wandered into the kitchen and Lana headed for the bedroom to find Purple Bunny. She could sure use him right now.

Only, he wasn't in his accustomed place on her bed, and she couldn't find him anywhere. What could have happened to him? And how could she get him back before some other disaster occurred?

Biting her lip, Lana joined her mother in the kitchen.

"What's wrong?" Serena asked.

"Nothing." Her mother had never understood about Purple Bunny.

"Then come, let's talk."

Lana sighed. She knew that look. Her mom was all set for a nice, cozy discussion. Ever since Lana's father died, her mother had focused everything on her only child, and had come to depend far too much on

Lana for company. Most of the time, Lana didn't mind, but right now she wished her mother would get a life of her own and stay out of hers.

Serena bustled around the kitchen, opening doors and peering in cupboards. "Where's your coffee, dear? Are you out?"

"I threw it away. The caffeine isn't good for the baby." Or so the Pregnancy Police assured her. "There's some decaf."

"I can't drink that stuff. I'll just bring some real coffee over and leave it here."

Lana preferred not to be tempted, but her mom wouldn't understand. Then again, maybe it wouldn't be too difficult to resist. Ever since Lana had realized there was a new life growing inside her, she'd been extra careful about what she put in her mouth. With Auntie Om's knowledgeable advice, Lana found herself searching out natural foods, baking her own bread, making her own jam and even mixing her own lotions and creams. She rather enjoyed getting back to the basics. It felt right, natural.

Lana poured her mother a cup of herbal tea, ignoring Serena's grumbling, then joined her at the kitchen table.

"All right, dear," Serena said, "tell me what's wrong. And don't fob me off with that excuse about Jimmy Bartlett's cigar."

Cupping her hands around the mug for its warmth and support, Lana said, "Okay, Mom, but are you sure you want to hear the truth?"

"Of course I do."

"Did you meet Blake Warner?"

"Yes, someone introduced me. He's the nice young man in construction, right?"

"Yes, and he's also the nice young man who fathered my baby," Lana said dryly.

Shocked, her mother exclaimed, "But you just met!"

"Well, no, we met five months ago. He was the stranger I met in Las Vegas." What was her mother thinking—that Blake was a sperm donor? "The baby happened in, uh, the usual way."

"Oh. Oh, dear. Why is he here?" Serena's hands fluttered in agitation.

"I don't know. This is the first time I've seen him since that night. And we didn't get a chance to talk with all those people around."

"So, he doesn't know..." Serena trailed off, her hands stilling and her face lighting in hope.

"No, he doesn't know he's the father. In fact, he thinks I'm married to the father."

"Well, if he doesn't know..."

Lana sighed. This time she would not be swayed. "Mom, I have to tell him."

"But the scandal—"

Exasperated, Lana said, "It's bad enough that I've been living a lie for the past four months. Now that Blake's found me, I have to tell him the baby is his. I don't care about the scandal."

Her mother patted Lana's hand. "I know, dear, but are you sure this is the right thing to do?"

"What do you mean?"

"I mean, how is Mr. Warner going to react to the news?"

Lana's shoulders slumped. "I have no idea." She wished she did. It would make things so much easier. "All I know is that telling him is the right thing to do. After that…'' She shrugged. ''I'll do what's right for the baby, that's all I know.''

Serena frowned. ''You don't want to do anything rash, dear, until you find out how he feels. When are you going to tell him?''

''As soon as I find him.''

''Hank mentioned he's staying at the Sky Hook.''

''Good—I'll give him a call.''

Lana headed for the phone and her mother made an awkward gesture. ''Would you like me to…leave?''

''You can stay. I'm not going to tell him on the phone, for heaven's sake. I just want to set up a meeting.''

''All right,'' Serena said and listened in as Lana placed the call to the Sky Hook.

''Hello, Hank. Could you get me Mr. Warner, please?''

''Well,'' Hank said, drawing it out. Lana could almost hear him scratching his chin. ''Afraid I can't do that.''

''Why not?''

''Lots of people been bugging him. He tol' me not to bother him for any more local calls.''

''But, Hank, this is important.''

''Sorry, Lana, no can do. He's my customer and the customer is always right.''

Lana rolled her eyes in exasperation. She knew that stubborn tone in Hank's voice—he'd never give in. She wished he'd put phones in the rooms so she wouldn't have to go through this. ''Okay, then I'll just come over and see him. Which room is he in?''

''Well…''

"If you don't tell me, I'll knock on all the doors until he answers."

"Now, Lana, you don't want to go doing that. He's in room three, only he's not there right now."

"He's not?"

"No, he tol' Esther he was gonna drive around some. Said the folks were bothering him and he needed to think."

Needed to think, did he? Well, Lana was going to give him a whole lot more to think about. "Will you let me know when he comes back?"

"Now, Lana, that would be invading his privacy."

Like Hank and Esther didn't? Lana knew exactly how those two operated—they were the biggest busybodies in town. No doubt Esther was watching Blake's every movement, grilling him on his comings and goings.

She frowned and Serena snatched the phone out of her hand. "Now see here, you old buzzard. Blake's a good friend of Lana's and he'll be glad to talk to her." She must have been satisfied with the answer she got on the other end, for she said, "Humph," and handed the phone back to Lana.

"You didn't tell me you was a friend of his," Hank said in an accusing tone. "I didn't know you knew him that well."

Ignoring his obvious fishing for information, Lana asked, "So you'll let me know when he comes back?"

"I don't know. He might not be back until late. I wouldn't want to bother you when you need your sleep for the baby."

The Pregnancy Police strike again. Lana rolled her

eyes, preparing to argue, then realized it was useless. "Never mind. I'll just leave a note on his door."

Unfortunately, there was no guarantee Blake would talk to her even if she parked on his doorstep. And with Purple Bunny missing, she couldn't count on luck giving her a hand. *I'll just have to take drastic measures then.*

Picking up the phone, she dialed Aunt Ona Mae and said, "Hi. Can you keep a secret?"

BLAKE RETURNED EARLIER than he'd planned. He'd hoped the peace and serenity of the falls and the beautiful countryside would distract him, but it hadn't helped. Everywhere he went, he pictured Lana, wondering if she'd played in this meadow, or sat on that rock and contemplated the stars.

Blake kicked himself mentally. Now that he knew she was married, it should be a lot easier getting her out of his system. This was what he wanted, wasn't it?

Ignoring the disappointment, he reached the motel room and found a note pinned to the door. *Please call me before you leave. It's very important.* It was signed by Lana and gave her phone number.

Blake crumpled the note and tossed it in the trash. It was no use. What could they have to say to each other? He glanced around the little room, which seemed a lot more suffocating and cheerless now.

He was too restless to work, the television held no attraction, and he'd finished his book. Now what? He doubted a weeknight in Bachelor Falls would contain much excitement. To kill time before he hit the sack, he decided to buy another book and grab a late dinner. But first, he needed to call Grace.

He entered the tiny phone booth behind the registration desk and closed the door in Esther's interested face. When Grace answered, he asked without preamble, "Can you book a flight for me tomorrow?"

"Sure," she said in a puzzled tone. "But why? Didn't you find her?"

He'd hoped to get away without being grilled, but should have known better. "Yes, but there's no point in staying."

"Why not?"

"Because she's married to another man and expecting his baby," Blake said.

"Oh." Grace paused, then said, "That would put a damper on things, wouldn't it? Hold on while I check the computer for available flights." After a long wait, she said, "Looks like the earliest I can get you out is tomorrow afternoon. Will that do?"

"Sure." It would have to. He wrote down the flight numbers and times, then said, "I'll see you tomorrow."

"Okay, but...I'm sorry things didn't work out."

"Yeah." So was he. "Thanks. Goodbye."

He hung up, told the inquisitive Esther he was going out for a stroll, and walked the short distance down to the main street where he remembered seeing a drugstore and diner. He pushed open the door of the drugstore and a woman he vaguely recalled meeting at the shower beamed at him.

She ran over to shake his hand. "Thank you so much. What you're doing is great for the town—just what we need."

Before he could ask what she meant, she scurried out the door, throwing him a little wave over her shoulder. Blake shrugged. Bachelor Falls seemed to have more than its share of eccentric personalities. He'd be glad when he could get back to the relative normalcy of Dallas.

He perused the limited selection of books and picked up a legal thriller he hadn't read yet. As he approached the cash register, Ona Mae stopped talking to the teenage boy behind the counter and stepped aside to give Blake room.

It appeared her fifties' attire was a permanent affectation, a personal quirk. Everyone else seemed to ignore it, so Blake did, too. He smiled at the boy whose name tag read *Josh* and took out his wallet.

Indecision warred on Josh's face as he rang up the purchase. He hesitated, then handed Blake his change and leaned over the counter to confide in a low tone, "I don't make much money here."

Wondering why he'd been singled out for such a confidence, Blake just nodded.

Apparently encouraged by this small sign, Josh blurted out, "I need more to get into college. Would you give me a job at your resort?"

Blake paused in the act of replacing his billfold in his back pocket. "What resort?" He searched his mind for the closest. "The one in Dallas?"

"No, the one here."

"But there isn't one here."

"I mean when you build one."

"I'm sorry," Blake said gently, loathing to burst the boy's bubble, "but I'm not building one here."

Josh turned away, disappointment clear on his face. Blake shrugged and left the drugstore, with Ona Mae right behind him. Once out the door, she tapped him on the shoulder, saying, "That wasn't very nice."

"Excuse me?"

She glared at him. "If you didn't want him to work for you, you should have just said so. There was no reason to lie."

She stalked off before Blake could respond. What was with this place? Did they exist in some kind of mind warp that made sense only to them? He'd be glad to get out of here tomorrow, back to the real world.

Shaking his head, he continued down the street to Hazel's Hash House where the bell on the door announced his arrival. As if it were a signal, the half-dozen people inside all stopped talking to stare at him. Feeling as though he'd entered the twilight zone, Blake nodded at them then headed to the counter.

The waitress swiped the counter with a rag and slapped a glass of water and a menu in front of him. She glared at him. "You been out to the falls?"

"Yes," he said and picked up the menu, hoping to hide behind it.

"Humph. Thought so."

To discourage conversation, he gave the menu a cursory glance and said, "I'll take the special."

"Good," she said with a decisive nod. "You won't be sorry. We serve the best damn food in Bachelor Falls—plain and good. Not that fancy stuff you sell at them resorts."

Wondering what he'd just ordered, Blake tried to be diplomatic. "I'm sure you're right."

She harrumped again but moved away to give his order to the chef. His relief was short-lived, however, because the four men in a nearby booth rose to their feet and headed his way.

Blake took a sip of water, trying not to make eye contact, but they approached him anyway. One man slid a business card on the countertop right under Blake's nose where he couldn't miss it. Sighing, Blake read, *Jake's Plumbing*. He eyed the man who had put it there, presumably Jake.

Jake said, "If you need a plumber, just call." Then, ducking his head in embarrassment, he hurried out the door.

Uneasily, Blake wondered if there was something wrong with the pipes in his motel room. Did Jake know something he didn't?

The three remaining men formed a loose semicircle around Blake. He smiled but kept his guard up, prepared to make a break for the door at any moment.

The short, pudgy man with an unlit cigar clenched between his teeth hitched up his pants and said, "I hear you're planning to dam up the river, get rid of our falls."

"Well, no—"

"It'd be a shame, 'cause of the legend and all."

Blake must have looked blank, for the cigar-wielder said, "You know, it's hard to have a town named Bachelor Falls with no falls. And without Bachelor Falls, you can't have bachelors, so the poor slobs'll have to get married."

"Excuse me?" Blake said, not comprehending.

"Naw, I done tol' you," the one in the middle said. "Progress is good. It'll make more jobs and bring money to the town."

The cigar-chewer pointed his stogie at the other. "Easy for you to say. You're married. Besides, progress isn't all it's cracked up to be. Not if it ruins the countryside and forces unsuspecting bachelors to get hitched."

They both cast pitying glances at the remaining big

blond man, then headed out the door, still arguing. Blake shook his head, wondering what that was all about.

The recipient of their pity regarded him with a half smile. Blake forced himself to lift the corner of his mouth, wondering what lunacy this guy was going to start spouting. Nothing too weird, he hoped. The guy was built like a truck, with muscles straining at the seams of his tight shirt. Not the type of guy you wanted to tick off.

"Hi," the man said and stuck out his hand. "I'm Ned Laney, the school coach."

Blake shook his hand. "Blake Warner."

"Yes, I know," Ned said, and gestured toward a stool on the counter. "Mind if I join you?"

Blake shrugged, not wanting to be rude.

Ned regarded him with amusement. "You looked a little confused there."

That was the understatement of the year. With a little hope that Ned, who seemed normal enough, could translate for him, Blake said, "What the heck were they talking about?"

Before Ned could answer, the waitress shoved a plate in front of him, muttering, "Bet that's the best damn meat loaf *you'll* ever have."

Blake glanced down at his plate. Meat loaf, mashed potatoes and green beans. He hadn't had this in years.

"She's right, you know," Ned said.

"Huh?"

"It *is* the best meat loaf you'll ever taste. Hazel has a way with meat loaf." When Blake just stared at him, Ned added, "Go ahead, eat. I've already had my dinner."

Blake took a bite and his eyebrows rose. It *was*

good. He swallowed and nodded. "You're right." He lowered his voice, deciding to take a chance that Ned was as normal as he seemed. "But is she always this belligerent?"

"No, but there are two diners here already. She just doesn't like the idea of more competition."

"I don't understand."

"Your resort," Ned explained. "It's bound to have an upscale restaurant in it and Hazel's afraid she'll lose business."

"Wait a minute. What's this about a resort?"

"You build resorts, don't you?"

"Yes, among other things."

"And you're building one here in Bachelor Falls, aren't you?"

The strange conversations suddenly made sense. "No. Where'd you get that idea?"

Ned looked surprised. "It's all over town. Why else would you be here? You're from Dallas, you don't have relatives in the area, and you've been up to the land next to the falls that Old Man Feeney has for sale. What else could it be?"

Wondering what else they'd learned about him, Blake muttered, "News sure travels fast. I'll bet you even know what color underwear I'm wearing."

Ned nodded. "White."

Blake stared at him. They *were* white.

Ned laughed. "Hey, come on, I'm kidding. Just a lucky guess—you gotta admit the odds were in my favor."

Relieved, Blake took another bite and chewed thoughtfully before swallowing. "Yeah, I guess. But that's not why I'm here. I came to, uh, visit a friend. But I...changed my mind."

"About building a resort?"

"I never planned to build one in the first place. I don't know how that rumor got started."

Ned nodded. "I thought as much. Rumors have a way of flying around this place, with little or nothing to back them up."

"So you'll set everyone straight?"

"No, I'm afraid I can't do that," Ned said with obvious regret.

"Why not?"

"It'll never work. They'll never believe me. Nope, they'll just go on believing what they want to believe and get all het up about it."

Blake shrugged. "That's their problem."

"It's yours, too. You started it."

"Me? How?"

"Just by showing up. You'll have to set them straight."

"Why? They'll figure it out when the resort doesn't get built."

Ned looked disappointed in him. "How long do you figure it'll take before they finally believe there's no resort? Two years? Three? You have to nip this in the bud, before folks get their feelings hurt."

"How am I supposed to do that?"

"Well, there's an emergency town meeting tomorrow night to discuss the Bachelor Falls Resort. You have to come."

Rolling his eyes at the realization they'd already given the nonexistent resort a name, Blake said, "But I'm leaving tomorrow morning to catch an afternoon flight."

"Can't you stay a little longer?" Ned asked. "I think you owe it to the town to set them straight."

Blake grimaced. Just what he needed—another person telling him what his duty was. But, damn it, Ned was right—Blake did feel responsible. And he'd already planned on taking a week off anyway, so it wasn't as though he didn't have the time.

"All right," Blake said grudgingly. "But I'm leaving after that. I won't be held responsible if they don't believe me."

"Fair enough," Ned said with a grin. "Thanks—I appreciate it."

Blake stared down at his dinner. He'd better eat it fast if he didn't want it to get cold. But first, he was curious about something. "What's this got to do with being married?"

Ned chuckled and explained the legend of Bachelor Falls and the antics that went on during the Bachelor Daze festival while Blake ate.

"I see," Blake said when Ned was finished. "How'd this get started anyway?"

"They say that when prospectors came to this part of the country sometime back in the 1800s, they used to shower in the falls once every few months before coming in to town to whoop it up. But the women wouldn't have anything to do with them because the shower turned their skin green."

Blake chuckled. "How'd that happen?"

"Who knows? Maybe something in the soap combined with the local plants or something. Anyway, some of the guys started showering on purpose to keep from having to get married and it kind of evolved into the legend we have today."

"And it's always worked?"

"Well...they always have a logical explanation if it doesn't."

"Convenient." Then remembering something that had puzzled him earlier, Blake added, "So why did those guys look so sorry for you?"

"I didn't shower during the last Bachelor Daze, you see, so I'm a marked man," he said with a rueful smile.

Blake grinned. "You mean some old maid tackled you and tied you up on the way to the falls?"

"No, I did it on purpose," Ned admitted. He paused, then said, "There's a woman I've been courting for a long time. I figured if I missed the shower, she'd get the hint and say yes."

"Did she?"

The rueful smile appeared again. "No, she married someone else instead."

"Hey, I'm sorry, man," Blake said in real sympathy. He knew how Ned felt, having received that punch in the gut recently himself. "So are you going to marry someone else?"

"I'm not interested in anyone else. But the legend can't be proven wrong. Either I get married before the next Bachelor Daze or I'll be ostracized by the entire town. I might even have to move."

Blake shook his head at the oddity of small-town attitudes and clapped Ned on the back. "Well, good luck with whatever you decide. I'll see you tomorrow."

He paid for the meal and walked back to his motel room, pausing only to tell Hank he'd be staying another night. Not wanting to risk running into Lana or arguing about nonexistent resorts with irate residents, he holed up in his room with the book he'd bought, ignoring anyone who knocked on the door.

He ventured out as little as possible the next day,

eating lunch and dinner at Mabel's Diner. It was on the other end of town, but Mabel was friendlier than Hazel. Either she hadn't heard the rumor, or she was just more polite.

When it came time for the meeting, he made his way to the town hall, which was packed with residents. It figured—he was probably the only entertainment around. Some folks glowered at him, some smiled, and all of them stared. He scanned the crowd, looking for a neutral place to sit.

As he did, he felt someone tug on his sleeve. He turned and gazed down into Lana's upturned face. His stomach lurched. Just the person he was trying to avoid.

"I need to talk to you," she said in a low voice.

"Now?" he asked in disbelief. He couldn't imagine what they had to talk about.

She glanced around. "No—after the meeting. Please, it's *very* important."

He couldn't resist the pleading in her face. What would it hurt to talk? She couldn't be any stranger than the rest of Bachelor Falls. "Okay, after the meeting."

She gave him a relieved smile and Blake fled. That smile had been his undoing before and he didn't want to give himself a chance to screw up again—not when all he wanted was to skim his hands over her lush curves, drown himself in her femininity.

He frowned. He didn't have the right to do that. That right belonged to another man, and Lana was carrying that man's child. He glanced around and caught a glimpse of Ned across the room. Relieved to find a friendly, normal face, Blake hurried to Ned's side.

"Glad you made it," Ned said. "I saved you a seat."

Blake sat and almost groaned in frustration. The chairs were arranged in a big semicircle around a podium and table, and Lana was sitting directly across the circle from him, watching him.

He heard the banging of a gavel and turned toward the front in relief. The stogie-chomping man who'd confronted him the evening before was evidently the mayor, Jimmy Bartlett. He called the meeting to order and announced that the primary topic of discussion was the Bachelor Falls Resort, then threw the floor open for discussion.

Following *Robert's Rules of Order,* Blake stood to be recognized, but it was useless. Everyone spoke at once, shouting out pros and cons of the mythical Bachelor Falls Resort. Mr. Robert would have thrown his hands up in disgust.

No one could be heard above the din, so Blake strode to the podium, plucked the gavel from the surprised mayor's grasp and banged it on the podium until everyone quieted down. "I'm Blake Warner of Warner Construction and I came here this afternoon to tell you there is no resort." That caused more uproar so he banged the gavel again until the noise died down.

"What do you mean?" someone yelled from the back.

"I don't know how the rumor got started, but I'm not planning to build a resort here."

"Then who is?" someone else shouted.

"No one, to my knowledge." Blake took a deep breath. "It's just a rumor—an *unfounded* rumor."

"Oh yeah?" his detractor shouted. "Then why *are* you here?"

Forcing himself to avoid looking at Lana, Blake said, "Personal business."

"Like what?"

Before Blake could inform the man it was none of his business, Lana stood. "He came to see me."

The room filled with the rustle of everyone's head swiveling to stare at Lana in surprise. "We met...a few months ago when I went to California," she explained.

She looked so embarrassed, Blake felt compelled to intervene. "Yes, I, uh, arrived unexpectedly and when I saw she was married, I thought it would be better if I just left."

Ned looked surprised and a lot of heads nodded throughout the room. Taking advantage of their understanding, Blake quickly added, "So, you see, there never was a Bachelor Falls Resort."

Everyone fell silent and Jimmy plucked his gavel back from Blake's unresisting fingers, saying, "Thank you for clarifying that. Now, if there's no further discussion—" He broke into a lopsided smile as a man slipped into the back of the hall. The mayor raised his voice. "Well, it's about time you came home."

Blake heard the whispers start and run around the room.

"Johnny Taylor..."

"Lana's husband..."

"Why didn't she tell us..."

Blake stood transfixed. Lana's husband?

The big, handsome man with a short haircut and a wide smile said, "So this is where everyone is! I thought the town was deserted. Are you all too busy to welcome back a native son?''

''It's about time,'' an old woman scolded. ''You need to treat your wife better than that.''

Johnny smiled sheepishly. ''So Lana told you.''

''Of course she told us.''

''Then, I'd like everyone to meet...'' He reached behind him and pulled a small, exquisite Asian woman through the door. She looked up at him with an adoring expression. ''...My wife.''

Pandemonium filled the hall as everyone bombarded him with questions, but Blake's eyes were riveted on Lana. He wondered how she'd take the news.

Not well. As he watched, she swayed on her feet and turned a sick shade of green.

Chapter Four

Lana felt the blood drain from her head. *Not now.* Not when the whole town—and Blake—were watching. She shot her mother an accusing glare. This is what came of lying.

As chaos reigned around her, Lana's knees buckled and her mother helped her back into the chair. She could do nothing but watch with a sick feeling of dread, knowing what was coming. If ever she needed Purple Bunny, it was now.

"What's going on?" someone shouted at Johnny.

They all quieted down when Johnny raised his arms for silence. "I got married," he said with a grin. "What's so strange about that? I missed showering last Falls Day, didn't I?"

"But you married Lana."

"No," Johnny said with a puzzled look. "I married Keiko."

Gasps echoed around the hall and one outraged citizen said, "You married someone else after you got Lana pregnant?"

Johnny's brow furrowed in confusion. "Pregnant? Lana's pregnant?"

Johnny's wife was beginning to look upset, so it

was time for Lana to bite the bullet. She stood, and bless her, her mother stood with her, hugging her as if to protect her from the world, her hands fluttering like mad.

All eyes turned to them and Lana gave Johnny a sickly smile.

"Tell them it's not my baby," Johnny said with a pleading look.

Lana took a deep breath, then said, "It's not his baby."

He sighed in relief but another murmur ran around the room.

"It's nice of you to protect him, Lana," a voice cried out, "but the man's gotta be made to live up to his responsibilities."

A chorus of assent followed, and Lana raised her voice to be heard above it. "I'm not saying it to protect him. He *isn't* the father of my baby. It's all a mistake." She went on to explain about flying out to meet Johnny only to learn he was married, landing in Las Vegas and Aunt Ona Mae's misunderstanding.

Comprehension appeared on most of the faces. Everyone in Bachelor Falls had been a victim of Auntie Om's misinterpretations at one time or another. Lana finished by repeating, "Johnny is not the father of my baby."

Diane Leftwich rose to her feet. A newcomer to Bachelor Falls, she was a divorced woman whose daughter was in Lana's class. Diane's strident tones rose above the shocked voices of the townspeople. "You mean you lied to everyone?"

This is what Lana had been dreading. There was no getting around it. She'd lied—and she had to own up to it. She gulped, then said, "Yes."

Her mother's supporting grasp tightened. "But only because I made her do it," Serena cried out. "She wouldn't tell me at first who the father was, so—" She broke off, clamping a hand over her mouth.

Lana's heart sank. If only she'd told the truth in the first place, she wouldn't have had to go through this pain. Expressions of hurt and condemnation appeared on her friends' and neighbors' faces as confusion erupted again.

The mayor banged his gavel for attention and looked sternly at Lana. "If Johnny's not the father, who is?"

Serena shot him an exasperated glance. "If she wouldn't tell me, what makes you think she'd tell you, you old buzzard?"

There was a titter of laughter, but everyone still watched Lana, obviously waiting for an answer. This wasn't the time or the place to inform Blake he was the father of her baby. Lana just shook her head, refusing to meet his eyes or anyone else's.

Diane's voice rose in a screech. "She doesn't know! She can't even tell us who fathered her baby." She pointed an accusing finger at Lana. "Well, I for one don't want that woman teaching my daughter. Lord only knows what foul and corrupting things she'll do to the children. Mayor, you're on the school board. I insist you fire her."

Aunt Ona Mae rose to her defense, poodle skirt swaying as she shrieked, "It wasn't her fault. The Bostians—" She broke off as Kelly dragged her back into her chair, whispering fiercely.

Lana winced and tried to sink back into her own chair, but her mother wouldn't let her. "Nonsense,"

Serena said. "Lana was only doing what I told her to, what she thought was right for the baby. You can't fire someone for that."

"But she's an unmarried mother," Diane said. "What kind of example will that set for our children? She has to be fired."

The black looks were directed at Diane this time. She'd said the wrong thing. No one in Bachelor Falls liked to be told what to do, especially not by someone they still considered an outsider.

Tall, lanky Bill Parsons rose to his feet and glared at Diane. "If all she needs is a husband, I'll marry her."

In the silence that followed, Ralph Nutley rose and declared, "Or I will."

Ned Laney rose also. "You know I will."

"Ditto," young Josh said with a grin.

The subsequent chorus of "Me, too's" was gratifying. Even the mayor and old Jasper spoke up. Lana felt her throat clog with emotion. The entire town had closed ranks to protect her from the outsider, and every unattached bachelor in Bachelor Falls had offered to marry her. Every one, that is, but Blake.

BLAKE WAS STILL TRYING to take it all in as he stared at Lana in shock. He tried to catch her eye, but she wouldn't look at him. Could it be?

Frantically, he tried to recall that night. It wasn't hard—the memory had been burned into his brain. Though all of his senses had been utterly occupied, it had seemed somewhat surreal, like a fantasy sequence or a perfect glimpse of heaven. Who worried about something so mundane as birth control at a time like that? He'd been so caught up in Lana and the sensations she'd aroused in him, he'd just...forgotten.

If he'd thought about it at all, he would have assumed she'd taken care of it. But...could it be? Was he the father?

He couldn't believe it. He'd had unwanted responsibility thrust on him all his life, and was very careful to avoid entanglement in other people's problems, other people's lives. Now, for one brief, irresponsible act, would he be forced into taking on even more commitments?

The thought chilled him. Not now—not when he was so close to obtaining everything he'd always wanted. He had to find a way out. The child couldn't be his. After all, Lana hadn't identified him as the father, and there were all these other men ready and willing to take on the responsibility. Surely *he* wouldn't be expected to do so.

Slowly, he came out of his self-absorbed fog and realized the townspeople were still arguing about who Lana should wed. Someone called out, "Let Lana choose. Pick one, Lana."

Lana blushed as all eyes turned to her and she jerked her head in a gesture of negation.

"Wait a minute," the mayor said. "You're forgetting something. We all showered in the falls last year. We can't get married."

"Sure you can," one of the men said. "After the next Bachelor Daze festival. All you have to do is wait until then, and not shower...then you'll be eligible."

Blake shook his head in amazement. These people certainly took their legend seriously.

The woman who had accused Lana said, "That's too late. She needs a husband now."

"Well," the mayor said, "you can see why she'll have to wait."

"No, she won't," someone called out. "Ned can marry her. He didn't shower."

"That's right," someone whispered and a murmur of approval rose from the room.

The mayor looked surprised. "I'd forgotten. Yes, Ned has to get hitched before the next festival anyway. We'll arrange it right away."

Everyone turned to look at Ned, standing next to Blake. Ned nodded, saying, "I'd be happy to."

What else could the poor man say when confronted by a town full of people pushing him into it? Poor bastard, forced to wed a woman he didn't love while the one he did was forever beyond his reach.

Blake turned to see how Lana felt about all of this. She gave Ned a half smile before she swung her gaze toward Blake. The combination of speculation, pleading, and anguish in her gaze solidified his suspicions and all of a sudden, the sure knowledge punched him in the gut.

The baby is mine.

Every fiber of his being recoiled in protest. No—this wasn't the way it was supposed to happen. *He* wanted to choose the woman who would become his wife. *He* wanted to decide when and where he'd have children. *He* wanted to control his own life.

Blake glanced at Ned, whose face had turned expressionless. Ned was a good man—he would make an excellent father. But could Blake let him take the rap? No, he couldn't. Blake wouldn't be able to live with himself if he had Ned's unhappiness on his conscience. He knew what he had to do.

This was his problem, his obligation. He'd brought this on himself in one moment of irresponsibility and now was the time to pay the price and take on the load. Blake was good at that—he'd had lots of practice.

What was the matter with him? This is what he'd wanted, wasn't it? Not quite. He'd wanted to get to know Lana better, but not this way. Not by force. Well, it looked like they didn't have any choice. He eased to his feet, trying to prolong the inevitable. Lana glanced at him with a mixture of hope and horror in her eyes. He wasn't sure what it meant, but it didn't matter. He knew his duty.

"There's no need for Ned to marry her. I will." That was it. Now the words were out and he couldn't recall them. He could almost feel the additional weight settle on his shoulders.

Shocked looks greeted his announcement and the mayor said, "Why? You just met."

"No, actually, we met five months ago." He paused before he dropped the final, irrevocable bombshell. "That's my child she's carrying."

LANA FELT HERSELF blanch as all heads swiveled to regard her. She willed herself to be calm. These adrenaline surges couldn't be good for the baby.

"Is it true?" someone asked.

Speculation, shock and avid curiosity met her gaze. Well, no matter what they thought, this wasn't something she planned to discuss in public. "I need to speak to Blake in private," she said, ignoring the questions.

"Tell us," Melva called out.

Serena turned on her. "It's none of your business, Melva Whiffington." She sniffed. "How would you like to have *your* daughter's life discussed in public?"

Incensed, Melva called back, "Well, *my* daughter would never—"

"That's enough, ladies," Ellie said. "Let them talk alone before you descend on them like vultures."

Everyone looked a little guilty, so Lana took advantage of their momentary lapse into good manners. Silently thanking Ellie who had to be as curious as the rest of them, Lana motioned for Blake to follow her toward the back of the hall.

He hesitated a moment then followed her. She could feel the eyes of the entire town boring into her back as she led him to what used to be a dressing room in the back of the old theater. Now it was just used as a storage room for odds and ends, but it was big enough to accommodate the two of them, plus it had the added advantage of a door, which would allow them a measure of privacy.

Blake shut the door behind them and pulled two chairs out of the stack on the side, urging her to sit. She did so, and stared at him, wondering what to say. In all the ways she'd envisioned telling him, none of them had included broadcasting it at the town meeting.

He stared back with a solemn expression and asked, "Is it mine?"

"Yes, it is. I'm sorry, this isn't how I intended to tell you...or the town."

He grimaced. "I'm sorry for announcing it like that...I don't know what came over me."

She smiled. "Bachelor Falls can do that to a person."

"Ah, that explains it."

They shared a rueful smile and Blake continued, "I had no idea or I would have returned your call last night."

"Why didn't you?" If he had, much of this mess could have been avoided.

He shrugged. "I thought you were happily married with another man's child on the way. There didn't seem much point in seeing you and dredging up the past—what little of it there is."

Lana felt her skin flush. "I'm sorry, that's my fault, too. When I learned I was pregnant and couldn't find you, Mother insisted I let Auntie's misunderstanding ride. I tried to track you down in California and Las Vegas, but couldn't find you."

"That's because I live in Dallas. I was just on a business trip."

"Oh."

His gaze searched her face. "I'm sorry if I caused you embarrassment. I guess I just got carried away. Everyone else was declaring themselves, so it seemed like the thing to do."

Lana smiled at the look of confusion on his face. "It's okay. You don't have to marry me."

"But I should have done something to prevent conception—the child is my responsibility."

Lana's heart sank. If that's all it meant to him, then she'd better disabuse him of his overworked sense of obligation right away. "It's mine, too. This baby has two parents—two people who didn't think about the consequences of their actions."

Lana blushed, remembering how right it had felt to

be in Blake's arms. How could something that felt so right be wrong? "It was irresponsible of both of us, but I don't regret it," she said softly. "Something very special came of our union."

A peculiar expression crossed Blake's face as he stared down at her protruding tummy. "I...I wish I'd known earlier, so I could have been here to help you with the decision."

"There was no decision to make. I couldn't do anything but keep my baby."

He looked as though he wanted to say something, but shook his head.

"I've always wanted children," she said, trying to explain. "Of course, I had planned on having them with a husband, but—"

"Don't worry, you will," he said with a determined expression. "I said I'll marry you."

And no doubt resent it, and them, every moment thereafter. She didn't want that for her baby. "It's all right, you needn't," she said gently. "I release you from all obligation." Better to raise the baby by a single loving mother than in a strained, two-parent household.

He squared his shoulders and glared at her. "I always live up to my obligations."

Saddened, Lana wondered what had happened to the man who had made such sweet love to her. He had been tender, loving, funny—nothing at all like this grim-faced statue.

Realizing she'd hit on some obscure point of male pride, Lana offered him another out. "If you want to take on some sort of financial obligation, I'd appreciate it." She didn't make much as a teacher and a little extra money would come in handy to take care of her baby's needs. "But you don't have to marry me."

The flash of hope that lit his eyes hurt. So much for her dreams of a loving family. She spoke mentally to the life inside her. *Don't worry, honey. We'll do just fine on our own.*

The hope on his face faded, to be replaced by resolve. "No, the baby needs a father, and a Warner always lives up to his responsibilities. We'll be married just as soon as I can arrange it."

And she had nothing to say about it? A little annoyed at his highhanded ways, she said, "But you don't have to be that father. Ned offered to marry me." Not that she'd take him up on it—she couldn't give Ned the love he deserved. And the other men in town would be relieved to be let off the hook. Lana knew, even if Blake didn't, that they had only offered to marry her in order to close ranks against the outsider.

"Another man shouldn't have to pay for my mistake."

Mistake? Is that how he saw their baby? Well, that settled it. She didn't want to marry a man who saw her baby as a mistake. "It won't be a hardship for Ned," she said without vanity. "He's been asking me to marry him for years."

Surprise registered on Blake's face. "He has? Then...you're the woman he's wanted to marry for so long? I thought she was married..." He trailed off, then snapped his fingers. "I see—he thought *you* were married."

"Right."

"Why didn't you marry him?"

"Because I don't love him." Did he think she was desperate to wed any man?

"But you're willing to marry him now?"

Avoiding a direct answer, she said, "He would make a good father." He would, too, but she didn't think she could do that to him. No, she wanted to hold out for mutual love. Blake didn't need to know that, though. After he left Bachelor Falls, she need never see him again. All she wanted to do was ease his mind so he wouldn't bother her with his talk of obligation.

Blake thought for a moment, then shook his head. "I can't let you do it. This is still my duty. I'll marry you."

So much for giving him an out. "Well, what if I say no?"

"What?"

"It's my decision, not yours."

He looked surprised, but just then a tap came on the door. The mayor stuck his head inside and said, "Are you through talking yet?"

"No," Blake said.

"Yes," Lana corrected him. "There's nothing else to talk about." Before Blake could argue with her, she swept out the door to deal with everyone else.

She made her way back to the podium, feeling weary. There was nothing like having her entire life on public display to make her wish she lived somewhere else, anywhere else. She felt like fleeing and taking all her cares with her, but she knew the townspeople meant well. They really did care about her and what happened to her baby...for the most part. And if she didn't take care of this now, they'd just badger her until she told them everything they wanted to know.

Or worse, they'd make something up.

Lana took a deep breath and looked out at the expectant faces of her friends and neighbors. Blake took up a position behind and to her right and Lana almost smiled. Her knight might be a little tarnished, but he was still trying to protect her back.

"What's your decision?" Melva called out. "Who you gonna marry?"

Blake stepped forward, saying in a deep, strong voice, "It's my child. She's going to marry me."

Lana winced at the note of doom in his voice, and felt a little irritated that people didn't seem to think she was able to think for herself. Why did they assume she had to have a husband?

Her gaze sought Ned's. His expression held concern and compassion, and he must have seen her wince, for he stood again, saying, "Is that true? Is he the father of your child?"

Lana nodded, feeling herself blush.

Ned smiled at her. "Whatever Lana decides is fine with me. But I would be more than happy to make her my wife."

Ned was always so kind. It was too bad he didn't make the blood sing through her veins. And too bad Blake didn't love her as Ned did. She just wished she could have the best of both men. She opened her mouth to deny them both, but was cut off by a voice from the crowds.

"She has to marry Ned," the mayor said. "He didn't shower in the falls last year."

"Don't be silly," Melva said. "If Blake's the father, then she has to marry *him*."

"No," Lana began, "it's my decision—"

"But Ned's gotta marry anyway," Jimmy protested. "The legend says so. And there's only a month left until the next festival. If he doesn't marry Lana, who will he marry? He's been drooling after her forever."

Embarrassed for Ned, Lana cast him an apologetic glance. He shrugged, but didn't deny it.

Melva rose to do battle. "Ha! That silly legend. You men have been using it as an excuse for years to avoid marriage."

The mayor pointed his stubby cigar at her. "You believed in it right enough when Joe didn't shower and your daughter saddled him with a ball and chain."

"Yeah," another man said. "You just don't want Lana to marry anyone."

There was a grain of truth in that, because of Melva's feud with Lana's mother.

"That's not true," Melva insisted. "The legend has outlived its usefulness. It's about time you learned that showering or not showering in the falls has nothing to do with marriage. In fact, it's pure hogwash," she said with an emphatic nod of her head.

Gasps greeted her proclamation, but Lana could see women's heads nodding all around the room.

Jimmy's face turned purple. "Name one time when it hasn't held true," he demanded.

"What about Dicky Simon?"

The mayor snorted. "Hell, that boy may have been over eighteen age-wise, but he sure weren't mentally. That don't count."

"Then how about Bob Jenkins?"

"Why, he hadn't even lived here a year yet, so he wasn't a proper resident. He don't count, either."

Melva sniffed. "You'll always find excuses, won't you?"

"No," Aunt Ona Mae shouted, flailing her arms to get their attention. "I tell you, it's the aliens."

This was degenerating fast. "Wait a minute," Lana called out, but the battle was on and neither side would be denied.

Ignoring both Ona Mae and Lana, the mayor said, "There's no excuses involved and the legend has held true for over a hundred years. What do you say to *that?*"

Melva grinned. "I say it was about time it was proven wrong. And it will be if Ned doesn't marry Lana."

"But he has to." At Melva's look of disdain, Jimmy added, "It will be a good marriage. They have lots in common. They're both teachers, they live in Bachelor Falls, they like the same things...why, they're perfect for each other. What do Blake and Lana have in common?"

"A child," Melva snapped.

The fight started in earnest then, polarized by gender, with the men insisting she marry Ned and the women insisting she wed Blake. Lana's efforts to get their attention were in vain.

Blake leaned close to her and asked, "Do you want to leave?"

"Yes," she answered, "but I can't until this is cleared up."

He nodded and stepped forward to grab the gavel then pounded it until he had everyone's attention. "Quiet, please. Lana has something to say."

All eyes turned to her, and Lana took a deep breath, then said, "I thank you all for your concern, but I want to make one thing clear. Who I marry is *my* decision and no one else's."

Another babble of voices broke out, insisting she was wrong. Serena rose to stand alongside Lana and hugged her daughter in a protective embrace. "She's right. It's her decision. Let her make it."

Ned and Blake, bless them, followed Serena's example. "I'm willing to accept Lana's decision, whatever it is," Ned declared.

"Me, too," Blake seconded.

Lana felt better with all this support, but knew it wouldn't last as soon as they heard what she had to say.

Again, all eyes turned to her. "Well," someone called from the back, "what *is* your decision?"

"I choose...neither. I'll raise my baby alone."

More gasps reached her ears and Lana felt the surprise of her supporters as the crowd called out their opinions.

"You can't do that!"

"You have to marry."

"The baby needs a father."

"The legend—you'll destroy the town!"

Lana banged the gavel this time until there was silence. "I *can* make that decision and I will. In fact, I just did."

The mayor gave her a stern glance. "Wrong. You have to marry one of them."

"Why? There are lots of single mothers these days."

"Not in Bachelor Falls. What kind of example is that for our young people?"

Lana thought cynically that he was using the very argument he'd decried earlier. How convenient.

He slapped his cigar in his mouth and clamped down, saying, "You either marry before the next festival or..."

"Or what?"

"Or you're fired. Then how will you support your child?"

Chapter Five

Blake concentrated on his morning routine, trying to avoid brooding about yesterday's events. It didn't work for long. When he ran out of distractions, he went to the lobby phone booth to call Grace. "I need to change my flight again," he told her.

She hesitated. "Again? It isn't like you to be so indecisive. What's going on?"

"Nothing, I just—" He broke off. Why lie? If anyone could keep a secret, it was Grace. He sighed. "No, that's not true. You remember the woman I came to see?"

"Yes."

"Well, she's pregnant."

"I know—you told me that earlier."

Blake clutched the phone tighter, unable to explain. It was dumb, but speaking the words aloud made it seem so much more real somehow.

"Blake?" Grace asked in the continuing silence. "I don't understand. What's going on?" Then, her breath catching as understanding dawned, she said, "Wait. Are you trying to tell me...*you're* the father?"

Actually, that's what he'd been trying *not* to tell

her. He should have known Grace would guess. "Yes."

"Are you sure?"

"Yes."

"Oh. Well, that puts a different spin on things."

"*That's* the understatement of the year." He fell silent again, willing the churning in his stomach to go away. Lana was the one who was supposed to get morning sickness, not him.

"Uh, you want to talk about it?" Grace asked, concern evident in her voice.

He did…and he didn't. "Maybe." His feelings were so mixed up, he didn't know what he thought.

"It might help if you talked about it. You know, solidify your thoughts and impressions on the matter."

Blake relaxed. That's what he liked about Grace. She was so logical and focused, so unemotional, that it was almost like talking to another man. Only better, because he didn't have to worry about what he said around her. "I don't know where to start."

"Well, maybe you can start by telling me why you're staying."

Wasn't it obvious? "She's having my baby, for crying out loud!"

"Not right this moment, surely," Grace said with a hint of laughter in her voice.

Blake saw nothing humorous in the situation. "No."

"Ah, I see," Grace teased. "You want me to coax it out of you. If multisyllable words are too difficult, I'll just play twenty questions and you can answer with grunts. One grunt means yes and two means no, okay?"

"Very funny."

"The man can talk," she said with feigned excitement.

"Forget the sarcasm, will ya? I need help here."

Grace's voice turned serious. "I know, but I can't help if you don't talk to me."

He sighed. "All right. What do you want to know?"

"Does she expect you to marry her?"

"No." And that was the problem. She wasn't reacting at all as he expected. Why couldn't she be like other women in this matter? It would sure make it easier.

"Ah, but *you* expect her to marry you, don't you?" Grace knew him well. "Yes."

"How do you feel about that?"

"What does it matter? It's my responsibility. I know my duty."

"Did you tell her that?"

"Yes."

"Well, I bet that made her feel great," Grace said, sarcasm dripping from her voice.

"What do you mean?"

"No wonder she doesn't want to marry you. You bungled it royally."

"How? I did what I was supposed to. I offered to marry her."

"Yeah, I know you. You probably wore a martyred expression and blathered some nonsense about honor and duty while you nobly offered her the protection of your name."

"So?"

Grace chuckled. "I knew it. The woman's *pregnant,* for heaven's sake—"

"I know that," Blake spat out, frustrated. "That's the problem."

"She's going through a rough time, Blake. She needs support and encouragement, not lectures. Hormones run amok in pregnant women—they're emotional, not logical."

"Not Lana." She was the coolest thing he'd ever seen.

"I'll bet."

"No, it's true. After the entire town attacked her last night, she was calm and collected and sassed them right back." He'd been impressed despite himself. "She's no pushover."

"Maybe not, but I'll bet she went home and cried her eyes out."

Why did that thought bother him so much? "Maybe," he said, unwilling to concede she might be right.

"What did you mean, the town attacked her?"

He explained the mix-up with Aunt Ona Mae and Johnny. "Every bachelor in Bachelor Falls offered to marry her because she wouldn't tell them who the father was. That's when I figured out I was the father, so I...told them."

"You told the entire town?" Grace asked, disbelief and laughter evident in her tone.

"It seemed like the right thing to do at the time," he said lamely.

"What about the others? Did she accept any of them?"

"No, but she said one guy—Ned Laney—would make a good father, and he wants to marry her."

"So you're off the hook."

"I know." It was too much, too soon. He'd wanted

to date her, not wed her, and the possibility of an escape was seductive. "But I don't think Lana wants to marry him." Besides, the thought of Lana with any other man was somehow distasteful.

"What about Johnny?"

"He's already married, remember?" Besides, Johnny was leaving town in two days.

"Who *does* she want to marry?"

"She says no one. She wants to raise the child by herself."

"Well, that's gutsy," Grace said. "But you sound like you don't believe her."

"I don't know what I believe. But that's irrelevant—she's a teacher and the school board insists she marry, or she'll lose her teaching job."

Grace let him know her opinion of small-town mores in no uncertain terms. As she vented, Blake held the phone away from his ear, waiting for her to calm down.

When she did, he said, "That's why I need to convince her to marry me. I grew up in a home with only one parent, for all intents and purposes. I know what it's like and I don't want that for my child. My child will have the best," he said in a stubborn tone. "A loving home."

"*Will* it be loving?"

"Of course I'll love the kid." How could she think he wouldn't?

"A good home needs more than that. Do you love Lana?"

"I don't even know her!" he protested. Suddenly the dam burst and all his feelings came pouring forth. He desired her, sure. What sane man wouldn't? She was curvy, even more so now that she was pregnant with his child, and utterly feminine.

Feminine with a mystery that pulled at him, making him want to discover all her secrets. She was strong, too—just look at how she'd stood up to everyone with that little smile that shut her and the baby in and the whole world out.

"Blake?"

"Sorry, she's got me in a tailspin."

"Ah ha!" Grace exclaimed in triumph.

"What's that supposed to mean?"

"Nothing," she said, though she made no attempt to hide the amusement in her voice. "How does she feel about you?"

"I don't know." How could he? Lana was so closemouthed, he had no clue. He still felt a wallop in his gut every time he saw her, remembering the brief time they'd spent together. Sure, it'd been almost five months ago, but it was branded on his memory forever.

"Go talk to her, then."

"Yeah, right. What am I supposed to do? Walk up and ask her if she's in love with me?"

"Why not?" Grace countered.

"We hardly know each other."

"You knew each other well enough to make a child together."

He didn't know how to respond to that.

Luckily, Grace didn't expect an answer. "You have to explain why you want to be involved in the life of your child. Make her understand, and by doing that, you might come to understand her, too."

Involved in the life of his child. Until Grace said that, Blake hadn't consciously realized how real this was. Out of Lana's body would come a little human being, complete with ten fingers, ten toes and a driving need to be loved.

The sheer thought of the responsibility made him balk, but memory of his childhood overcame it. Yes, he wanted to be involved, watch his son or daughter grow up surrounded with love and attention. He wouldn't have it any other way. "I—I don't know where she lives."

Grace heaved an exasperated sigh. "That's just an excuse and you know it. It's a small town. Ask the motel manager. He'll probably know."

Yes, Hank seemed to know everything that went on here. "Okay, okay. I'll talk to her." He paused to think. "Uh, did you tell my parents I was coming back early?"

"No, I haven't mentioned it yet."

"Good, don't. Looks like I might be gone longer than I expected. Can you handle things there?"

"Sure."

"Good. And...keep this to yourself until I work everything out, okay?"

"You got it. Oh, and Blake?"

"Yeah?" The amusement in her voice was becoming annoying.

"Keep me posted, will you? This is even better than a soap opera."

"Yeah, sure," he said sourly and hung up. He was glad someone was getting some entertainment from this situation.

LANA HAD JUST GOTTEN comfortable after a hard day at work when the doorbell rang. She sighed. She'd gotten so many calls with well-intentioned advice, she'd taken the phone off the hook. She'd hoped that would deter the majority of the people, but apparently some were so anxious they had to beat a path to her door.

She peered through the peephole. Ned Laney. Well, she supposed she'd better speak to him.

He came in with an uncharacteristically tentative smile. "I tried to call, but—"

"I took the phone off the hook."

"Oh. Lots of calls, huh?"

She rolled her eyes. "That's an understatement. It seems this is everybody's baby but mine. They all think they know what's best for me."

He smiled, asking, "So, what do they think is best?"

"Well, so far, it's running neck and neck. The men think I should marry you and the women think I should marry Blake." She paused.

"Even Ellie and Kelly?"

Lana sighed and ushered him into the kitchen, tossing over her shoulder, "No, they're just ticked at me for not telling them before everyone else knew about it. They'll back me in whatever I decide."

Lana poured him a cup of coffee just the way he liked it, and they sat down at the table together—she with herbal tea, he with coffee.

Ned gave her a look full of compassion. "So will I, Lana."

Her heart filled with tenderness. Ned was really a good friend. "Thank you."

He glanced down at the cup, his hands curled around its warmth. "I meant it, you know. I still want to marry you."

"You'd be willing to raise another man's child as your own?"

"For you, I would," he said softly. "Besides, you know I like kids."

Yes, and he was very good with them. Her gaze slid from his. "I—I can't do that to you."

"Why not? You know I've loved you for years, even when you were Johnny's girl."

She hadn't thought about Johnny in a long time, except as her mythical husband. Blake and the baby had driven her ex-fiancé from her heart.

Ned covered her hand with his tentatively, as if he wasn't sure of his welcome. "But you were always so untouchable then."

Untouchable...that's the way he had always treated her, as if she were some fragile porcelain statue to be put on a pedestal and worshipped. But she didn't want worship. She wanted love and passion...and down and dirty sex. Especially lately. Her dreams had become erotic, and all focused on Blake. *He* certainly didn't treat her as if she were untouchable.

Shaking her head, she brought her thoughts back to the conversation. She couldn't picture Ned getting down and dirty with her. He'd be too afraid she'd break.

She squeezed his hand. "Thanks, Ned. You have no idea how much I appreciate the offer, but...I'd hate to do that to you."

His mouth twisted in a grimace. "Hate to do what? Fulfill all my dreams?"

"No." How could she say this without hurting him? "I'd hate to marry you without loving you. You deserve better than that."

He sighed and nodded as if he'd expected her to

say something of the sort. "Well, Blake seems to be a good man. If...if you decide to marry him, I'll understand. I just want what's best for you."

Her heart filled with tenderness for such a wonderful friend, Lana led him to the door and kissed his cheek. "Thanks again. I'll let you know what I decide."

"All right—"

The doorbell rang again, startling them both. She groaned. "Now who is it?" Not up to answering more endless questions, she asked, "Could you deal with whoever that is and send them on their way?"

"Sure," he said. "It's the least I can do."

The open door blocked Lana's view of her visitor until Ned opened it wider, saying, "I think you'll want to see him."

Blake stood there, looking incredibly sexy with one lock of hair falling over his forehead and an expression of indecision on his face. Her heart rate sped up and she swore her hormones surged at the sight of him. Remembering, no doubt, how they had gotten down and dirty with *him.*

She glanced uncertainly at the supposed rivals for her affection, but they smiled at each other and shook hands. They were genuine smiles, too, and she could tell they liked each other as they exchanged polite greetings. She didn't know why she was so surprised. She liked both of them—why shouldn't they like each other?

Ned stepped aside and laughed. "I've had my turn. I guess it's yours now." He looked up. "Uh-oh. There's Auntie Om. I'll head her off. I hear there were marks that looked like a spaceship landing up by Old Man Feeney's barn."

Lana chuckled. "Thanks, Ned. I owe you one."

Blake grinned and let Ned pass, then called out a farewell as Ned took off down the walk toward Aunt Ona Mae. He turned back to Lana and his smile faltered. "Can I come in?"

"Of course."

He walked in, gazing around at his surroundings as she led him into the living room. She'd automatically taken Ned into the kitchen, but Blake rated the living room. Why? She supposed it must be the difference between a good friend and a good…what?

Maybe it was better if she didn't finish that sentence.

Blake sat down and smiled. "Your house looks like you."

She sat opposite him. "It does?"

He made a half-aborted gesture at the surroundings, appearing embarrassed. "It's feminine, natural, earthy and…comfortable."

Lana glanced around the familiar room, trying to see it through his eyes. Plump, inviting cushions in a multitude of pastel colors spilled over the soft floral sofa. Matching curtains hung at the windows, with warm scatter rugs covering the wooden floors. Plants in a variety of earthen containers flourished in abundance around the room, interspersed with cherished antique tables filled with candles and dried flower arrangements.

Yes, she supposed it could be termed earthy, feminine and natural. And it was comfortable, but she wasn't sure she liked that word applied to herself.

Unsure how to react to his statement, she just smiled. "Would you like some coffee?"

"No, thank you." He frowned at the cup in her hand.

"Don't tell me you're a member of the Pregnancy Police, too," she said.

Startled, he said, "Excuse me?"

"That's what I call the people who tell me what I can and can't do," she said in a challenging tone.

"Oh. Well, I don't think I have the right to tell you what to do."

Perversely, that hurt. Was he disassociating himself already from the child they'd made together? She glanced into her cup, hoping for answers from the tea leaves inside.

"Is something wrong?" he asked.

Ignoring the question, she asked, "Why are you here?"

"I think that's obvious."

"Maybe, but I've learned to take nothing for granted." Especially since the town's reaction had surprised her so much.

"I thought we should talk." He paused, then asked, "How do you feel about the ultimatum?"

She had nothing to lose by telling the truth. "Angry. But I understand why they issued it."

He nodded. "Have you made a decision yet?"

She eyed him skeptically, but he didn't appear to be pushing. Just curious. "Not yet." She was too overwhelmed to feel capable of making any rational decision at the present time. "None of the choices are ideal."

"What do you mean?"

"I want what's best for my baby," she said, her tone vehement. Her anger subsided at his understanding nod. "But I don't know what that is yet, though

I'm tempted to tell them where to shove their ultimatum.''

"Can you afford to do that?''

"Financially, no. But even if they force me to leave my job, I can find another one.'' The problem was, she didn't want another job. She loved teaching children. Spreading her hand across her unborn child, Lana said, "We'll do just fine.''

His gaze dropped to her stomach. "But wouldn't the baby be better off with a father?''

"Not necessarily. Even if he—''

"He?'' Blake echoed. "You know it's a boy?''

"No, I don't want to know until he or she is born. I just can't bring myself to call the baby 'it.'''

Blake nodded, so she continued. "As I was saying, even if he doesn't have a live-in father, the town will adopt him like they have Aunt Ona Mae.''

His brow furrowed in puzzlement. "Is that why she seems to be related to everyone around here?''

"Yes—the poor dear has never been right since her fiancé, Lowell Murtry, left her many years ago.''

Comprehension dawned on his face. "Is that when the, uh, aliens showed up?''

Lana chuckled. "Yes. The story changes often, so we're not sure if they were both captured by these Bostians or it was just her fiancé, but she's been seeing alien conspiracies ever since. She's convinced he's going to come back for her someday. That's why she dresses like she does, to keep herself the way Lowell remembers her.''

"Ah, I see. Whose aunt is she, really?''

Lana chuckled. "Believe it or not, I don't know. It's become a matter of pride here in Bachelor Falls. Everyone claims her as a relative and none of the old-timers will tell us for sure who she's related to. I've grown up believing she was my aunt, but so have all my friends.''

He gave her a bemused look. ''I didn't know towns were like that.''

''This one is.''

He nodded. ''But a town, no matter how caring, is still no substitute for a live-in father.''

''That's true.'' What was he getting at?

''Ned would make a good father,'' Blake ventured.

What about Blake? She stared down into her teacup. ''Yes, he would, but I don't love him.''

''He loves you.''

''That's not enough. I—I can't marry him when I don't love him. It wouldn't be fair to him. He deserves better.''

Blake rose to take her cup, then settled on the couch next to her and took her hand in his. ''I'd be a good father, too.''

Her heart flipped over in her chest. ''Would you?''

''Yes, I would. Why won't you marry me?''

She shrugged. ''I guess I'm a romantic. I want to marry for love—mutual love. Not convenience.''

He nodded thoughtfully, his thumb stroking the back of her hand in an apparent unconscious gesture that sent thrills of longing through her.

''We like each other,'' he said. ''And...we're attracted to each other.''

Definitely. She nodded, wondering where he was going with this.

''Maybe it will grow into love, given time.''

Maybe. She had a feeling it would be very easy to fall in love with Blake...but did he feel the same? She had to know more. ''That's not enough.''

''I—I can't promise I'll love you—''

''I know,'' she said, not wanting to hear the rest

of it. There was enough pain without it. "And I'm not asking you to."

He regarded her with a doubtful expression. "Whatever you decide, I want to be a part of this child's life."

Touched, she squeezed his hand back. "Don't worry. You will be. I'd never deprive you of that right. But..."

Concern grew in his eyes. "But?"

She blurted out, "*Why* do you want to be a part of his life?"

He looked surprised. "I know where my duty lies—" He broke off. "Why are you shaking your head?"

"Don't you see?" she appealed to him. "Children can sense things like that. If you want to see him merely out of duty, I'm afraid you'll hurt him. I want my baby to be loved."

Anguish twisted his features. "I *will* love the baby," he said. "It's just that duty is very important to me."

"I can see that."

"No, you don't see. I'm an only child, so my father constantly preached duty at me from an early age. I tried to avoid the family business, but ten years ago, there was an accident. My father's partner, my uncle, was killed and my father's injuries were too bad for him to work. I had to take over his company. Now I'm the sole support of my parents, not to mention a great many employees—and cousins."

Wondering why he was telling her this, and realizing they'd somehow achieved the same intimacy they'd felt on the plane, she said, "Go on."

He heaved a sigh. "All my life, I've had responsibility shoved on me. It wasn't my decision, and not what I would have chosen given the chance.''

"I see. And the baby is just one more thing thrust upon you without your decision.'' She understood, though she couldn't deny it still hurt.

He nodded. ''My father is no longer able to run the business, but that doesn't stop him from trying. Only a few more months, and I'll be able to win the bid for a major construction project. With that, I'll gain complete control and with my father out of the way, I can finally have some time off. You know, take a vacation or two and leave the company in someone else's hands without fear of him messing something up.''

His expression and voice turned wistful as he whispered, ''Only a few more months and I would have been free.''

Doubting he knew he'd spoken that last sentence aloud, she said, ''You still can be. I don't expect you to take on *my* burdens.''

He just shook his head and she knew he still felt them whether she absolved him or not. She squeezed his hand and changed the subject. ''What would you do if you were free?''

''Go fishing,'' he said with a rueful grin.

She chuckled. That wasn't the answer she'd expected at all. ''What kind of fishing?''

''I don't know. I've never been.''

''You've never been? Then how do you know you'll like it?''

''I don't. But I've never had the luxury of finding out.''

''Well, we'll just have to remedy that,'' she said, patting his hand.

''What?''

"Tomorrow's Saturday so I have the day off. I'll take you fishing."

"You will?" Slow delight spread across his face. "But I don't have a pole or...bait or...whatever else you need."

"Don't worry, I do. And I know the perfect spot. But I'll have to pick you up bright and early in the morning," she warned. "Like about five o'clock. And you'll need to stop by the hardware store to pick up a fishing license with a trout stamp."

He grinned. "No problem. But are you sure you want to do this?"

"Yes, of course. It will give us a chance to get to know each other a little better without the whole town watching."

"Then...you'll still consider marrying me?"

"I'll consider it," she confirmed. But it would be Blake's actions, not her thoughts, that decided the matter.

"Good. I'll—"

The doorbell cut off his sentence. Lana grimaced. "See why we need to get away?"

He chuckled and stood, saying, "Shall I tell whoever's at the door that you're...indisposed?"

"Yes, please. I'm not up to seeing anyone else today." And she had a lot to think about, too.

"Well, I'll see you tomorrow then, at five o'clock."

"All right. I'll look forward to it."

He grinned. "So will I. You have no idea how much."

Chapter Six

A knock came on the door promptly at five o'clock the next morning. It was still dark, but when he answered the door, Blake could see that, instead of wearing one of the flowing dresses he'd become accustomed to, Lana wore jeans with a T-shirt and jacket, her long blond hair scrunched up in a ponytail stuck through the end of a ball cap.

Somehow she managed to make even this prosaic outfit look sexy. He grinned at her. "Do the fish care if we get up this early?"

She cocked her head to regard him. "No, they don't, but you might. This is when they're biting." She smiled. "Besides, most people aren't up yet to see where we're going."

"Good point." The stares and whispers that followed him everywhere he went were a little disconcerting. He wouldn't mind escaping from them for a little while.

She glanced down at his feet. "New shoes?"

"Yes—I didn't want to ruin my loafers so I bought some tennis shoes last night." He grinned. "I may not have fished before, but I have a suspicion there might be mud or water involved."

She chuckled. "There usually is. Ready?"

"Sure." He shrugged on his jacket and followed her to the car. "Where are we going?"

"I know of a stream in a secluded place where we won't be bothered. It's a great spot for trout, too."

"Sounds good." He was surprised at how much he was looking forward to this. And surprised at his surprise. Wasn't this what he'd been wanting to try for years?

A surge of anticipatory joy surged through him. It was even better this way, without all the spontaneity planned out of it. He rolled down the car window and inhaled. The chilly predawn air wafted fresh scents of growing things to his appreciative nostrils, unlike the prevailing odor of hot asphalt and exhaust fumes he was accustomed to.

"How far is it?" he asked, anxious to begin.

"Not far." She slanted him an amused glance. "Are you sure you have the patience for fishing?"

"I don't know. I guess we'll find out."

"Fish aren't like your subordinates, you know. They won't come at the snap of your fingers." Her teasing tone took the bite out of the words.

She obviously didn't know the people who worked for him. "Really?" He feigned disappointment. "The way folks around here talk, I figured all I needed to do was hold out my arms and the fish would just jump into them."

She chuckled. "Well, you can't believe everything you hear." She pointed to his feet. "There's a thermos down there if you'd like some coffee."

He sighed in satisfaction and picked up the thermos. "Ah, a woman after my own heart."

A fleeting expression of pain crossed her face and

Blake berated himself for saying something so stupid. She followed immediately with a small smile, as if she meant to show him she knew he didn't mean anything by it. Relieved, he figured he'd be better off keeping his mouth shut and the rest of the ride passed in companionable silence.

As dawn broke, Lana pulled off the road down a dirt track to park in a wide spot near the stream. Blake helped her retrieve the tackle box and poles from the trunk and followed her down in the dawning light.

She indicated for him to stop when they reached the water, and he set down the gear, looking around him in enjoyment. Trees spread their leafy branches across the rocky stream, which flowed and twisted across the landscape. Birds twittered a welcome, insects skittered across the moving water, and a soft breeze ruffled the leaves as the sun began to warm the scene.

Blake smiled. "It's a beautiful spot."

Lana smiled. "My favorite." She pointed to the other side of the stream. "See that boulder?"

"Yes."

"Well, trout like to hide in the pool beneath it."

He grinned. "No kidding? You think we might be able to coax them out for breakfast?"

"Maybe." She handed him a pole and showed him how to attach a hook and sinker, then the bait.

Impressed at her deft handling of the unfamiliar objects, he teased, "No worms? Shucks. I always wanted to play with worms."

She smiled. "These salmon eggs are easier to handle."

He caught a whiff of them. "But I bet they don't smell any better."

She chuckled. "Maybe not. I don't think the fish care."

"Do you think we'll catch any?"

"Who knows? That's not the point of fishing, anyway."

"It's not?" Blake asked in surprise. "Then what is?"

Lana seated herself on a flat rock and motioned for him to join her. "Fishing isn't really a sport, it's a state of mind." She gazed out at the serene scene with a calm expression. "It's just you, the glory of nature, the pole and the fish you hope to entice."

"How do you entice them?" Blake asked with a grin. "Here, fishie, fishie?"

She slanted him a rather superior smile. "No, I think the bait will suffice."

She showed him how to cast his line and play the line back to tantalize the fish. He followed her instructions and his bait sank into the pool with a plop. He made himself as comfortable as he could on the rocky bank and watched the line for any sign of movement.

"Do we need to be quiet so the fish don't hear us?" he whispered.

She played out her line. "So long as you don't talk too loudly, it shouldn't be a problem. But you might want to try just letting go. Just be for a while." She leaned back against a rock and smiled at him. "That's what I do."

Just be? He'd never tried that before. "You do?"

"Yeah—sometimes I really need this."

"But you always appear so...serene. So together."

She smiled. "How do you think I get that way? Everyone needs some time to meditate, to clean out the cobwebs and stay centered." She raised her face to the rising sun and closed her eyes with a blissful smile. "And right now, I need that very much."

Of course she did. So did he, for that matter. Following her advice, he watched the water trickle over the rocks and eddy into the small pool. There, it lapped against the large boulder where, he imagined, a whole mess of fish hid, taking great delight in ignoring his bait.

Who cared? It was peaceful in this spot...so peaceful. He let his mind wander and a feeling of guilt tried to rise within him for all the work waiting back at the office, but he quelled it. There was no room for work here.

He pushed away anxiety about the future, concern about the woman next to him and annoyance at the town. Instead, he let himself drift like the current, pretending he was all alone in the world, with no one to bother him...no one to make demands on him...no one to dump responsibilities on him. He sighed in contentment as he felt muscles relax that he hadn't even known were tight, and became one with the nature all around him.

A few moments later, Lana reeled her line in. "Ah, just as I thought. The bait's gone. These fish are clever. You might want to check yours."

Blake's bait was gone, too. He rebaited the hook and cast his line out again, then reeled it back a little. Just as he was making himself comfortable once again, he felt a tug and saw the tip of his pole bob.

Excitement surged through him. "I think I've got something." He rose to his feet. "What do I do now?"

"Pull back sharply to set the hook."

He did so and let out a whoop. "It's still there!"

Lana grinned. "Keep the line taut and reel it back in a little at a time. Don't let it go slack."

He grinned as he felt the fish fight back. Following her instructions, he reeled in the trout until he saw it break the surface and its tail flash in the sun.

"Raise it up and bring it over here," she instructed.

He did as she said and the fish swung high, flapping in the air as he swung it toward Lana.

It missed her head by about an inch. She ducked. "Whoa, you're dangerous with that thing. Here, set it down in the shallows."

He somehow managed to finagle the wriggling trout to the spot she indicated so she could snag it with the net. Then, with great care, she showed him how to remove the hook and place the trout on a stringer.

He felt absurdly proud of his accomplishment. "It's a big one, isn't it?"

She laughed up at him, her eyes gleaming in the sunlight. "I hate to burst your bubble, but it's only about eight inches. I'd say that's about average."

He grinned and helped her to her feet, unembarrassed by his own enthusiasm. "Well, it's the biggest fish I ever caught. Of course, it's the *only* one, but..."

He trailed off as he gazed down at her. The woman who carried his child looked so warm and womanly and comfortable here in these time-lost surroundings. "Thank you for showing me this," he whispered.

Her answering gaze was tender. "You're welcome."

Their gazes caught and held, wondering and wistful as they shared the moment. Lana's lips parted and a question filled her eyes. Blake answered with a soft brush of his lips against hers.

She kissed him back, and he gathered her into his arms, cherishing the soft feminine feel of her curves, remembering what it was like to have her lush body bared before him. Desire rose within him but he tamped it down. That was what had caused their problems to begin with.

They pulled apart and her gaze slid away from his as she inquired, "Want some breakfast?"

He let her go and pretended the kiss hadn't meant anything, hadn't just beaten through his defenses to settle her forever somewhere around his heart. "Trout for *breakfast?*"

"No," she said, laughing, taking the bait. "I brought some muffins and bagels."

They munched on the pastries companionably and Lana regaled him with Bachelor Falls fishing legends. After one particularly tall tale, Blake laughed. He tweaked her ponytail, saying, "I haven't laughed like that in a long time. Thanks."

"So, you like fishing, huh?"

"Yeah." The sense of peace was incredibly soothing. Unfortunately, though, he could still sense the restraining bonds of his ignored obligations tugging at him, reminding him of his duties. It set up a renewed longing in him to be free, to break the shackles of his imprisoning life. "I wish I could stay here forever," he murmured.

Lana studied him, thinking if anyone needed the kind of peace and contentment this sport brought, Blake did. She grinned. "Ah. What you need is more fishing."

And he'd be better off doing it alone. She picked up her gear. "I'll head downstream a little ways.

Leave you alone with the fish...and your thoughts. Get to know yourself.''

She could see he meant to object, but she wouldn't let him. No doubt he had some chivalrous notion that he should protest that he wanted her company. ''I need to be alone a little while,'' she said. It wasn't strictly true—Blake was a great fishing companion—but she wanted to give him some time to himself without him feeling guilty about it.

She left him some tackle and moved down the stream until she found a comfortable grassy spot. Feeling a little tired, she decided to just lie there for a few moments and rest.

The next thing she knew, she was being wakened by water splashing on her face. *What the...?* She opened her eyes to see a grinning Blake shaking his wet hand over her.

''Is this a new fishing technique?'' he teased. ''Using z's for bait?''

''All right, you caught me,'' she said with a sheepish grin. ''I thought I'd lie down for a few minutes. I guess I fell asleep. Lately I'm sleepy all the time.''

His grin sobered at this reminder of her pregnancy. ''I didn't realize.''

''That's okay.'' She checked her watch. ''Good grief, I've been asleep for hours. It's past time for lunch. You must be starved.''

On cue, his stomach growled. He laughed. ''Guess I can't argue with that.''

''Well, I have some food in the car. Help me up, will you?''

He levered her to her feet and she brushed the leaves and twigs off, saying, ''How'd you do?''

''Great! The fish were really biting.'' He led her

back to his spot at the stream where he proudly pulled his stringer from the water. "Not bad, huh?"

He must have had ten fish on that line. "Not bad," she agreed and smothered a smile.

He glanced at the fish then at her. "What's so funny?"

"Nothing. Only...the limit's six."

The expression on his face was comical. "Limit? I didn't realize."

"They should have told you when you bought your license."

"What do I do now? I can't throw them back."

"It's okay. I haven't caught any so we're still two fish short of our combined limit."

"Good. They don't seem to be biting now anyway."

"They usually don't when the sun's so high. They'll start again when it begins to go down. So, let's eat." She brought out the sandwiches and chips. "Fishing's hungry work. And you never know if you're going to catch any or not."

"Aren't we going to eat them?" he asked.

"Not now—I didn't bring anything to cook them with." At his disappointed look, she added, "I figured we'd have them for supper. Sound good?"

"Sure. I love fresh trout and you can't get any fresher than this."

She took a bite of her sandwich and asked, "So, is fishing what you expected?"

"Yes. It's just what I needed." His wide grin and relaxed posture corroborated his simple statement. "But it can be kind of scary, being alone with my thoughts."

"Especially if you're not used to it. Would you rather do something else instead?"

"Yes, I think I've been alone with myself enough for today. Besides, I want to get to know *you* better."

"Okay. The day's yours. What would you like to do?"

"Avoid people."

Her smile widened. "Okay. That's easy enough to do. How about I show you the sights?"

He agreed, so after she taught him how to gut and clean the fish in the stream, they picked up a few things at the local K-Stop and packed the fish in ice. She drove him around to her favorite spots, including the breathtaking falls the town was named for and the spot where the single men showered on Falls Day.

Blake was a pleasant companion—not too talkative, not too quiet, so when the sun started to set, she was reluctant to go home. Instead, she headed farther away from town, hoping he wouldn't object to spending a little more time alone with her.

"Where are we going now?" Blake asked.

"My father built a cabin up here. We used to spend a lot of summers here before he died and I still come up here sometimes when I want to get away."

He smiled at her. "Sounds great to me."

She pulled up next to the rustic log cabin and unlocked the door. After she started the generator, she showed him the two small bedrooms, the kitchen, the dining room with its picnic bench table and the living room, dominated by a large stone fireplace.

"This is great," he said with enthusiasm. "Everything you need. Only, where's the bathroom?"

"Out back."

His eyes widened. "You're kidding. An out-house?"

She chuckled. "Yep—you're in the big time now. It's even a two-holer."

He dragged her out to see it, and she laughed at his delighted expression when he found the half moon her father had carved in the door.

"Satisfied now?" she asked, anxious to get away from the ripe odor.

"Not really. Where are the corncobs?"

She burst out laughing. "Shucks," she mocked in a put-upon accent. "We've moved beyond corncobs in these here parts. And since we don't have any catalogs, guess you're just gonna have to make do with toilet paper." She pointed to the roll on the wall.

"And here I thought we were roughing it."

"Oh, we are," she assured him with a grin. "It's generic paper."

"I feel much better now, thanks." His eyes twinkled, reminding her of the Blake she'd met on the plane.

"No problem. How about we cook those trout?"

They took the provisions out of the car and Lana showed Blake how to fry the trout in butter while she prepared potatoes and a salad to go with them.

When they finished eating, Blake looked down at his empty plate in surprise. "I didn't know I was that hungry. But everything tasted so good. I don't know when I've had a better meal."

Pleased with their comfortable companionship and Blake's enjoyment of the simple things, Lana said, "That's how it goes after fishing and hiking all day. And the clean air out here always seems to make everything taste better."

"I guess you're right." He glanced out the window at the night. "It's kind of a shame to be inside."

"We don't have to be."

"What do you mean?"

"Come on. Help me clean the dishes and I'll show you."

They finished cleaning up and Lana grabbed a flashlight and a quilt, leading him out to the meadow. She spread the quilt on the ground and lay on it, saying, "Come join me."

"Are we going to sleep out here?"

"No, we're just going to do some stargazing. Come on."

He lay down next to her with his hands behind his head and gazed up at the sky. "Wow. It's so bright. Everything is clearer out here."

"Yeah. Where's the Big Dipper?" They studied the stars for a while, trying to match star configurations with known constellations without much success. Neither of them knew much about astronomy.

"Look," he said. "A shooting star."

"Quick, close your eyes and make a wish." She followed her own orders, wishing fervently.

When she opened her eyes, Blake was propped up on one elbow, gazing down at her. "What did you ask for?" he questioned softly.

"I can't tell you or it won't come true," she protested. Besides, how could she tell him that her most fervent desire was for them to fall in love and make a family together, right here in Bachelor Falls?

He brushed a strand of hair from her face and gave her a searching look, serious and intent. "What do you want out of life, Lana?"

Her heart swelled at the tender look in his eyes. "I told you that in Las Vegas."

"A husband and children? That's it?"

"Well, maybe a dog, too."

He chuckled, and she added, "That's enough, if they're loving."

He smiled sadly. "I wish I could give that to you."

She did, too. She was already in love with this special man and wished he could feel the same about her...and their child. She stroked his cheek. "It's okay. You aren't responsible for me. Only *I* am responsible for me."

A troubled look crossed his face, and she could see he wished she were right, but he'd been taking care of everyone else for so long, he didn't know how not to.

"Trust me, Blake." And, just because she wanted to and it felt right, she pulled his head down to meet hers.

Their lips met and clung—a tender kiss full of heartbreak and unspoken need. She sighed and snuggled as close as she could, laying her head on his shoulder.

He gathered her in his arms and placed a soft kiss at her hairline. "You're something special," he murmured.

Contentment washed over her, flavored by hope and desire. "I am?"

"Yes, you're the most...sensual woman I've ever met."

She pushed him until he was lying flat on his back and she was gazing down at him. "Is that good or bad?"

He smiled and pulled the band from her ponytail,

letting her hair drift down to spill onto his chest. Playing with the strands he'd released, he asked, "Why would that be bad?"

"Some people find it...overwhelming."

He cocked an eyebrow. "People?"

She shrugged. "Men."

"Then they're idiots."

"Really? You didn't mind me using you as a sex toy in Las Vegas?"

He laughed out loud, startling her with his genuine amusement. "Is that what you were doing?"

"Well, yes."

"Then I was using you as a sex toy, too. It works both ways, and I didn't do anything I didn't want to do."

"You didn't?" she asked in a small voice.

"Hell, no. You're the most desirable woman I've ever met." His hands caressed her back and moved down to her behind where he stopped, the heat of his hand searing into her flesh. "What man wouldn't want you?"

Feeling daring, she whispered, "Do you want me now?"

"More than you know."

She ran her hand down below his waist, gratified to feel the hard evidence that proved he was telling the truth. His hand tightened on her buttock as she caressed him through the rough denim material.

"Lana..." he said in a broken voice.

She unbuckled his belt and popped the button to pull the zipper down on his jeans.

"Should we be doing this?" he asked.

"Oh, yes, I think we should." She wanted him more than anything she'd ever wanted before.

"But...the baby."

"It won't hurt the baby." Besides, she'd found the increased desire as a result of her pregnancy made this an imperative. She was more than ready for him.

And she loved the way he made her feel—special, sensual and very feminine. It give her a sense of power and control. Exercising that power, she glanced down to see his erection straining at the white cotton of his briefs then slid an eager hand under the waistband to caress his smooth skin.

He sighed. "That feels good. But we're both wearing too many clothes."

"So we are," she teased. "What should we do about it?"

"This," he murmured, and peeled her clothes away one by one. He made stripping her an erotic adventure of sensuality as his hands and mouth nipped, kissed, licked and suckled bare patches of sensitive skin...everywhere but where she most wanted him. More eagerly, she helped him off with his clothes until they were both lying naked to the stars.

The night air had turned chilly and she shivered as he stared down at her, running his hand over her hip and down her legs, still teasing her.

"Are you cold?" he murmured.

She nodded. "Make me warm." She grasped his hand and brought it to her breast, pushing the hard nub against his palm and willing him to touch her yearning nerve endings.

"Here?" he teased, plucking at her nipple.

"Yes," she exclaimed, then sighed as he bent his head to suckle first one breast then the other. Longing built deep within her as his hand moved down to delve between her legs. His soft caress, lubricated by the moisture of her body, struck to the very core of her being.

She reached for him, grasping his shaft to stroke the pliant skin over his hardness, wanting to give him as much pleasure as he was giving her.

"Wait," he said, stilling her hand.

"No." She guided him toward her waiting heat. "Please, I can't. I want you inside me."

With his tip nudging her slick opening, he said, "Are you sure?"

"Yes, I'm sure. I want you now."

He pushed inside and they both exhaled at once. She giggled at their simultaneous sigh of relief.

He paused to kiss her lingeringly. "Feels like home."

"Yes," she whispered, wrapping her legs around his waist. "Welcome home."

Their lovemaking was slow, sensual, filled with soft caresses and hot, wet kisses. Finally when she could stand the tension no longer, she thrust her hips upward to meet him, burying him deep within her. "Harder," she murmured.

He obliged, going faster and faster until the tension suddenly peaked and released in a flood of sensation that inundated her entire body. A moment later, Blake cried out his joy and they became one in ecstasy beneath the moonlit sky.

Ah, yes. Home, indeed.

Chapter Seven

Jimmy Bartlett banged his gavel on the podium to call the meeting to order.

"What's going on, Mayor?" Ralph Nutley yelled out. "Why did you invite only men?"

Others chimed in. "Yeah, and why the secrecy?"

"What's so urgent you had to call a meeting so early in the morning?"

"Just a minute and I'll tell you." He waited for the noise to subside. "A serious crisis is facing Bachelor Falls. One that requires every able-bodied man's attention."

He paused until he received the expectant silence he wanted, then continued in ringing tones. "If we don't do something and do it fast, the legend will be in serious jeopardy."

Someone at the back said, "Oh, is that all?"

His oratorical brilliance was lost on this crowd. "All?" he repeated. "*All?*" He glared around the room, picking out the bachelors for special scrutiny. "These women are man hungry. The only thing keeping them from descending upon you and wresting away your freedom is the protection of the legend."

"Ah, you're just worried about yourself. Afraid you'll have to get hitched to the widow Eubanks."

"You're right," the mayor confirmed. "I am worried." Jimmy valued his freedom and liked the arrangement he and Tommie Nell Eubanks had worked out. But he'd be damned if he'd live with a woman pushing and prying at him all the time. He'd avoided that ball and chain all his life, and he wasn't about to let some city slicker come in and jeopardize his cozy arrangement. "You should be worried, too."

Ned Laney stood. "I don't understand. What's the problem?"

"You're the problem, son. We need to get you hitched, and fast, or the legend's dead."

"You didn't seem so concerned about your single status the other night. Didn't I hear you offer for Lana?" Ned glanced around at the other bachelors. "In fact, every one of you did."

Jimmy squirmed. That was a momentary aberration he'd rather not remember. "Aw, we just did it to show that upstart Diane Leftwich a thing or two. You know we weren't serious." Before Ned could ask any more uncomfortable questions, Jimmy continued the attack. "Why didn't you shower last year?"

Ned frowned. "Unlike you, I *wanted* to marry Lana."

"But why didn't you ask someone else when you thought she was married?"

"She's the only one I want."

"Well, you might not be able to have her. Who's your second choice?"

"I don't have one. Besides, Lana isn't married yet. I still have a chance."

Jimmy pointed his cigar at the coach. "But you

only have a month to talk her into it.'' Wouldn't you know Lana would be the one contrary female in town? Any other woman would jump at the chance to hog-tie a fine, upstanding young specimen like Ned Laney. "You need to get moving on it, son."

Ned shrugged. "I asked her—what else can I do?"

"Woo her, boy. Go out there and woo her. Don't let that stranger steal a march on you."

The coach made a gesture of negation. "She's carrying his baby. I can't compete with that."

"You must try. For all of us. Why, I hear she and Warner spent the whole day together yesterday...alone. No telling what they got up to. You can't let this outsider steal your girl."

"Yeah," someone shouted. "We don't want him staying here and building no resort."

The mayor frowned him down. "There is no resort—you heard him say so."

"Then why are there two men out looking at Old Man Feeney's land?"

"I don't know, but Mr. Warner isn't here to build a resort. He came here to steal Lana...and we've got to stop him!"

He was gratified to hear cheers greet his exclamation.

"Wait a minute," Ned called out. "Don't do this for my sake."

"We aren't—we're doing it for the sake of every goldurn bachelor in Bachelor Falls. Since you're too wrong-headed to tie the knot with anyone else, we have to make sure Lana marries you or the legend will be dead. That means we have to get rid of Blake Warner or sabotage his chances."

"That's ridiculous. Besides, I don't want to win

that way." Ned glanced around, and could obviously see the men were on the mayor's side. "If you do this stupid thing, don't count on me. I'll have no part of it." When they didn't respond to his tirade, he stormed out.

After Ned's dramatic exit, Jimmy turned to the crowd and opened his arms wide. "We're doing what's best for him. He wants to marry Lana and we just want to help him do that...and save the town in the meantime."

Nods greeted his pronouncement, so he stuck his stogie back in his mouth in satisfaction. "Now, how are we going to go about it?"

THE BELL JANGLED over the door of Hazel's diner as Blake walked in for breakfast. All eyes turned toward him and he grimaced, feeling like a bug under a microscope. How did Lana stand living here?

Figuring a quick getaway might be necessary, he avoided all eye contact and slipped into a booth close to the door, facing away from the curious stares.

Hazel popped her gum and slapped a menu in front of him. "Coffee?"

"Yes, please."

She poured it and hesitated, glaring at him. Finally, she seemed to come to some decision and lowered her voice to say, "You're gonna do right by Lana, aren't you?"

Blake tried to fend her off with a cold stare, but it didn't work. She just stood waiting for his answer. Sensing she wouldn't go away until she got one, Blake said, "I asked her to marry me."

"She agree?"

"Not yet."

"Humph. Well, if you ask me—"

"I didn't," Blake said, interrupting her. The last thing he needed was advice from someone who knew nothing about him or his situation.

She raised her hands in mock surrender but didn't take offense. "Okay, okay. I gotcha. But if you need help, just call me."

He jerked his head in a single nod, then ordered breakfast and stared into his cup. Hazel took the hint and left. He sighed, glad to be left alone with his thoughts.

Or was he glad? He'd decided a brisk walk and breakfast might clear his head, help him figure out what he should do. Only it didn't seem to be helping.

He didn't know what it was about Lana, but every time he saw her, he couldn't keep his hands off her. Even now, when she was nowhere near, he wanted nothing more than to track her down, bury himself in her warmth and softness, and just tune out the rest of the world.

But that was impossible. In fact, the knight was in danger of slipping off his horse. He shouldn't have indulged himself last night. He'd asked her to marry him because of the child, but he knew what she really wanted was a loving husband and family right here in Bachelor Falls. It wasn't fair to make love to her and let her hope he was *in* love.

He'd never felt that emotion. Hell, he'd never had time. There were too many responsibilities and too many people counting on him to let himself do anything so whimsical.

But for one brief, foolish moment last night under the stars, he'd dreamed he could. Dreamed he could drop all his obligations, kidnap Lana and spend the rest of their lives in that little cabin of hers, fishing and making love.

Not necessarily in that order.

He sighed. It was impossible. He could never do anything so irresponsible and he knew it. Unfortunately, so did everyone else in his family...and the company. The only ones who didn't know it were the people in Bachelor Falls.

Would Hazel be so adamant about him "doing the right thing" if she knew he would need to steal Lana away to Dallas to do it? He doubted it.

"Can we join you?" came a voice behind him.

It was the mayor and one of his cronies. "Well, I—"

"Thanks," Jimmy said as he and his friend slid into the other side of the booth. "This here's Ralph Nutley," Jimmy said.

Blake sighed and nodded at Ralph. It looked as if he had company whether he wanted it or not. "What can I do for you, gentlemen?"

Jimmy chewed on the stub of an unlit cigar. "Nothin'. Just thought, seeing as how you're planning on marrying our Lana, we ought to get to know you a little better. Let you get to know us."

The short, skinny Ralph looked confused, but gamely echoed Jimmy's words. "Yeah, get to know us."

"I don't think that's necessary." He didn't plan on sticking around for long.

"Oh, I think it is. 'Specially seeing as how Lana needs so much help and all."

"Needs help?" Ralph echoed in a surprised voice. Blake felt movement under the table and the little man winced. "Oh yeah, help. She needs help."

What was going on here? Blake thought he'd probably regret it, but he asked, "What kind of help?"

"It's like this," Jimmy said, leaning in with an air of confidentiality. Ralph followed suit, and the two of them looked like a couple of conspirators from a B movie. Casting furtive glances to either side, Jimmy whispered, "She's not quite right...in the head."

A heaping plate of ham and eggs slid through the middle of the huddle to land in front of Blake. Hazel popped her gum and glared at Jimmy. "Who's not right in the head?" she asked in a belligerent tone.

"Lana," Ralph supplied, then winced again at another movement under the table.

"Why, that's ridiculous," she exclaimed. "Nothing's wrong with Lana."

"A lot you know about it," Jimmy growled. "Do you mind? This is a private conversation—man talk. Go bother your other customers."

"Well, I never," Hazel said and cast them a fulminating glance before she sashayed away.

"She don't know nothin'," Jimmy said. "This is known only to the city council. We've been keeping it a secret."

If they thought they were taking Blake in, they were sadly mistaken. Playing along, he asked, "What's her problem?"

The two men exchanged glances. "Well," Jimmy said. "It's like this. Lana's got a mental illness."

"Mental illness," Ralph confirmed, nodding his head.

"What kind of illness?" Blake asked, digging into his breakfast and preparing to be amused. This was a new variation on running the outsider out of town. Instead of scaring him off with the threat of tar and feathers, they were trying to frighten him with fairy tales.

"Her mother won't tell us exactly, but every once in a while, Lana just goes wacko."

"Wacko," came Ralph's confirming echo.

Blake choked back a laugh. He let his eyes widen with astonishment. "What do you mean?"

The mayor lowered his voice. "You know how she's into all that...natural stuff?"

"Yes."

"Well, she's into voodoo, too. She's been seen many a night dancing stark naked under the full moon, chanting wild songs and throwing herself around in a frenzy."

"Is that all?" Blake asked. "Hell, you see that in Dallas all the time."

Jimmy seemed taken aback for a moment, then said, "No, that's not all. She...chops off chicken heads and smears the blood all over herself." He lowered his voice again. "She's even been known to kill a pig or two and sometimes, when the moon is just right, I've even seen her eyeing plump little children." He nodded for emphasis.

Ralph stared at him with eyes wide-open.

"Hasn't she, Ralph?" the mayor said with a glower.

"Uh, sure, plump...children?" It was more of a question than a statement.

Blake took another bite to chew over their words and stifle his laughter. "Well, that's different," he said. "Decapitated chickens and pigs I could live with, but children, no."

Jimmy's mouth spread in a relieved smile. "That's what we thought."

"Yes," Blake continued. "You know, I wonder why you let her teach those plump little children." He took another bite and waited for Jimmy's reaction.

The mayor's grin faded, and Blake could almost see the wheels turning as he fought to come up with an explanation. "Oh, they're in no danger," he assured Blake.

"How do you know?"

"Because...because...we lock her up at night when the moon is full," Jimmy said in triumph. "You can't be too careful."

"No, you can't," Blake agreed solemnly.

"So I guess you don't want to marry her anymore, huh?"

Blake stroked his chin. "Oh, I wouldn't say that. It might be handy to have a wife who knows how to butcher livestock."

Ralph gazed at him in shock. "But your children, man. What about them?"

"Oh, I think they'll be safe enough. And I could always lock her up at the full moon, too."

Jimmy chewed on that for a moment, then said, "It's not *just* the full moon—"

"That's enough," Blake said. He was finished with his breakfast and with them. "You're lousy liars."

"But—"

"It won't work, so you might as well stop trying. Did you really expect me to buy that story?"

"Yeah," Ralph said with wide eyes. "I was kinda believing it myself." He winced, saying, "Dang it, Jimmy. Stop kicking me!"

Before Jimmy could make up anything else, Blake added, "You might as well give it up. I'm not going to believe anything you have to say now."

"But—"

Laying all his cards on the table, Blake said, "What we do with our lives is our decision. Not yours. If you'll excuse me, gentlemen?"

Jimmy grudgingly moved out of the booth and Blake dropped a couple of bills on the table, then walked out shaking his head.

What kind of sucker did they take him for anyway? Actually, he was kind of glad it had happened. Up until now, he'd been worried about taking Lana away from her home, but after this farce, he decided she'd be much better off in Dallas.

LANA ENTERED the town hall hesitantly, wondering why she'd been asked to the Sunday afternoon meeting of the secretive Bachelor Falls Women's Horticultural Society. Most of the members were women her mother's age or older, and new members had to be invited to join, or to even participate in their meetings.

There didn't seem to be many horticultural events coming out of the society, though, and Lana had often suspected the group of being nothing more than an excuse to gossip. At last she had the chance to find out.

The older women welcomed her and waved her to a seat in the circle. She knew all of them, but wasn't surprised to see Auntie Om missing. The secret society wouldn't be secret anymore if she were a member.

As Lana passed by the women, each turned into a Belly Buffer, patting her tummy with affectionate little gestures as she went by. Lana just smiled and made her way to her seat. Maybe it was her impending motherhood that made them invite her. Whatever the reason, she was anxious to see a meeting of this group. She'd promised Ellie and Kelly to report back on what she learned.

Tommie Nell Eubanks, a short, plump woman who still had a lot of beauty for a woman approaching fifty, stood and called the meeting to order, saying, "Thank you all for coming at such short notice. And please welcome our special guest, Lana Talbot."

The women clapped. Special guest, huh? Guess that meant she wasn't going to be asked to join. Lana smiled politely and waited to hear why she'd been invited.

Tommie Nell smiled back. "Without further ado, I'd like to turn this meeting over to Hazel to explain why we're here."

Hazel rose, still in her pink waitress uniform, and said, "The men are plotting against us. They had a secret meeting this morning and they wouldn't tell any of us anything—not even their wives."

The audience murmured and Lana could see heads bobbing in agreement. Amused, she wondered what the big deal was. Weren't they having a secret meeting themselves?

"But," Hazel continued in a triumphant tone, "I found out what they were up to."

Excited murmurs rose from the circle. "What did you find out?" Tommie Nell asked.

"Well, I overheard Jimmy and Ralph talking to Lana's young man."

"Blake?" Lana burst out. This was no longer amusing.

"Yes, Blake. They were telling him something was wrong with you."

"What?" Lana sat up straighter. "What's wrong with me?"

"I don't know. They was huddled real close and shooed me away before I could overhear anything else."

Outraged whispers rose from the group. Lana knew how they felt—she was experiencing quite a bit of outrage herself. "Why would they do that?"

"Well, I have a notion about that," Hazel said. "Seems to me they're trying to scare the boy away from you."

Indignant now, Lana asked, "Well, I know the town is a bit leery of strangers, but this is going a bit far, don't you think?"

"Oh, it ain't because he's a stranger," Hazel assured her. "It's because of the legend."

"The legend?"

"You heard them at the town meeting. They're afraid if you don't marry Ned, the legend will die."

"So they're trying to run Blake out of town?" Lana asked incredulously. "I don't believe it."

"It's true, hon. They'll do anything to keep that sorry excuse in place."

"That's right," Melva said. "Why, look at what Jimmy's been doing to Tommie Nell for years."

Tommie Nell flushed, and Melva said, "Well, it's true. We all know it. He's been finding excuses to shower every year."

Tommie Nell ducked her head and mumbled, "He said it was an accident."

"For six years running?" Melva said. "That's a mighty strange set of accidents that just make him 'happen' to take a dip in the falls every year."

"But—"

"Especially since he never seems to do it on any other day except the one that counts. Face it, Tommie Nell, he's using you."

Serena stood and shook a finger at Melva. "That's enough. You're embarrassing the poor woman. Sit down and don't be so mean."

The other women echoed her sentiments and Melva sat, frowning at all of them. "The point is, dear," Serena said to Lana, "the men want you to marry Ned to keep the legend alive."

"But he doesn't have to marry me," Lana protested. "He could marry anybody."

"Hellfire," Hazel exclaimed. "Everybody knows the boy's sweet on you. He ain't gonna tie the knot with anybody else until after you're hitched to Blake."

"Wait a minute," Tommie Nell protested. "What if she wants to marry Ned?"

All eyes turned to Lana and she grimaced. "Well, it's about time you thought to ask what I want."

"Well," Hazel demanded. "Do you want to marry Ned?"

"No, but—"

"What about Blake?"

That was a harder question. "I don't know."

"You don't know?" Melva repeated in a voice filled with sarcasm. "Well, *my* daughter always knows her own mind."

"Shut up, you old witch," Serena said. "Let her explain."

"Well, I never. Listen—"

"Hush," Hazel yelled. When she got the silence

she wanted, she said, "Let Lana talk." Turning to Lana, she asked, "Do you love Blake?"

She paused. She'd been falling in love with him ever since they'd met, and last night had sent her over the top, as if all she'd needed was the good lovemaking seal of approval. "That's not the point."

Hazel huffed. "I thought so—you love him. So why in tarnation don't you want to marry him?"

Embarrassed at being asked to reveal her emotions in public once more, Lana stared down at her hands. "I'm not sure he wants to marry me."

"He asked you, didn't he?"

"Yes, but only out of duty." Couldn't they understand the humiliation of seeing the man she loved forced into marrying her? "He doesn't really want to."

"No man *wants* to," Hazel exclaimed. "Just look at Jimmy. You know he'd be happier married to Tommie Nell, don't you?"

"Probably, but that doesn't mean Blake would be happier married to me. I mean, Jimmy and Tommie Nell have had a relationship for years. I've only known Blake a few months."

"Still, love is love. He'll come around. You'll see."

The women all nodded in unison. Even Melva and Serena were in agreement.

Lana couldn't let anyone else dictate her life. She stood, and said in a firm voice, "This is my decision, not yours, and I'm not going to marry Blake just to satisfy his notion of responsibility. I want my baby raised with love, not duty."

"But what about the legend?" Hazel asked.

Exasperated, Lana said, "I'm not responsible for the legend. If you let it control you and your lives, that's your problem, not mine. Just...don't put up with it."

"But—"

"I'm sorry," Lana said firmly. "What you do about the legend is your problem. What I do about my baby is mine." With that, she walked out the door before anyone could stop her. She knew what was right for her and her baby—they didn't.

The women watched Lana leave, then Hazel said, "She doesn't know what's right for her."

"Right," Melva agreed. "She loves Blake and he'll come to love her in time. That baby needs a father. We'll just have to make sure they get together."

"Yes," Tommie Nell said, her eyes gleaming. "And make sure Ned doesn't marry either. We'll beat this legend yet!"

Cheers greeted her announcement and Hazel said, "Whether she likes it or not, we need to do this for her own good—for Lana and Tommie Nell and all the other single women in town. Are you okay with that, Serena?"

Serena nodded, her mouth set in a grim line.

Hazel smiled. "So we're all agreed? We'll watch those wily old coots to make sure they don't scare Blake off, and do everything we can to get Blake and Lana together. We just won't tell Lana what we're doing."

A chorus of affirmation sounded around her. "Good," Hazel declared. "She'll thank us later. So will our daughters and descendants and every single woman in Bachelor Falls from now to the end of eternity!''

Her ringing tones seemed to galvanize the society, but a lone voice spoke up from the back row. "Yes, but don't tell Ona Mae. She'd ruin everything.''

Chapter Eight

Blake smiled as Aunt Ona Mae leaned down to inspect the dead bolts he'd just installed in her doors. "You sure these will work?" she asked.

"Guaranteed to keep out all known alien species," he assured her. It didn't hurt to pander to an old woman's eccentricities. She had a good heart and other than a couple of small peculiarities, she was perfectly normal. In fact, he was becoming rather fond of her. "I use them and I've never had a single alien slip through."

She peered up at him. "Easy for you to say. They're not after *you.*"

"Are you sure they're still after you?" he asked. "You haven't seen any in a long time, have you?"

"No, but I hear 'em. Last night I heard a scratching sound at my door, like they're trying to get in." She clawed at the door to demonstrate the proper alien motion, then lowered her voice to a whisper. "They won't go back to Bost without me."

It was probably just the neighborhood cat, but if it made Auntie Om feel more important to be the object of a demon's demented desire, Blake doubted he could say anything to change her belief. "Don't worry. These locks will keep them out."

"Humph. We'll see."

She showed him out and he smiled when he heard the dead bolt slam shut. She was taking no chances.

He made his way back to the motel, hoping to have some time to himself. He'd been kept busy for days since Jimmy and Ralph had tried to con him. On Monday, he'd helped Hank replace paneling in one of the motel rooms. On Tuesday, the mayor had asked him to review some plans for the beautification of Bachelor Falls. Much to his surprise, the plans really did need review and Blake spent all day showing them how they could cut costs without sacrificing quality and have a more efficient design.

Wednesday, Jake asked him to help out with a large and dirty plumbing job at the local Save-Rite grocery store. Today, Blake had already helped Hank with landscaping in the morning, and Ralph had talked him into installing Aunt Ona Mae's locks this afternoon.

He found it difficult to say no, especially during Lana's work hours, even though he suspected the sudden desire for his services was a plot to keep him away from her. Except...all of those jobs really did need doing, with the possible exception of the alien-deterring locks.

He entered the motel, wondering if he could sneak in and call Lana before someone else caught him.

No such luck. Hank appeared out of nowhere, saying, "There you are. You got a phone call."

Resigned, Blake entered the tiny booth to answer the phone. He hoped it was Lana, but didn't expect it. He'd had a hell of a time trying to get her alone in the past few days. "Hello?"

"This is such an antiquated setup," Grace said on the other end. "I can't believe it."

"Oh, hi, Grace." Surprisingly, Hank closed the door and left him alone in the little room.

"What's wrong?" she asked. "You don't sound happy to hear from me."

"Oh, it's not that. It's just that the town seems to be conspiring to keep Lana and me apart."

"Conspiring? How?" She sounded delighted.

"I'm glad this is amusing you."

"Yes, well, I don't get out much," she said with a chuckle. "Your situation is the only entertainment I've had lately—it's like something out of an old movie. So, tell me what they're doing now."

"It's just that I can't get Lana alone. Every time I try to see her, she has to work or somebody shows up to talk to her about the baby or ask me construction questions. It's as if the men have suddenly decided I'm Blake the Builder Buddy. I told them what they really needed is a town manager."

Grace chuckled. "It's not as bad as that, surely."

"You have no idea. I can't even talk to her on the phone without making it a town event. Everyone keeps sticking their heads in to ask silly questions or to insist they need the phone right away to make an important phone call."

"Aren't you being a little paranoid?"

"No, I don't think so. They only bother me when I talk to Lana—not you or anyone else. In fact, I suspect she's called a few times and Hank just hasn't told me."

"Well," Grace said, "then you won't mind coming back to Dallas early."

"Why? What's wrong?"

"It's the Palladian resort jobs. They've moved the bidding up two weeks."

"Why?" Blake demanded. "Never mind. Let me think." Getting the bid on this project was the key to winning control of the company. And with the resort being built in his stomping grounds, he had the edge. He knew the Dallas construction industry backward and forward, and had already lined up the premier subcontractors. The only thing he hadn't done was complete the bid proposal package. He'd figured on having a month to complete it when he got back. Now he only had two weeks.

"There's more," Grace said. "Since you're not here, your father is getting involved in the bid proposal."

Damn it—the man was supposed to be retired. Why couldn't he keep his fingers out of things? He might have known the construction industry ten years ago, but not today. He'd just mess things up with his old-fashioned attitudes.

That decided him. "I'll be there. But, damn it, I haven't resolved things with Lana yet."

"Ask her to come with you, then."

"That's not a bad idea." It would get Lana away so he could talk to her, and give her the opportunity to know Dallas at the same time so she'd get used to the idea of living there. "I'll see—"

A knock on the door interrupted him. "Hold on," he told Grace. "Let me see who's here now."

Esther poked her wizened head through the door, and with a furtive glance over her shoulder, whispered, "Serena's just told me Lana's at the diner if you want to see her." She put her finger to her lips.

"Shh. Don't tell Hank I told you." She cast a glance over her shoulder. "Oh, no, he's coming now."

"Thanks," Blake said to the closed door.

"What was that all about?" Grace asked in an amused tone.

"Oh, just one of the locals telling me where Lana is. I'd better go find her and see if she'll come to Dallas with me."

"Would you like me to book two seats for you?"

"Yes, but keep hers flexible. She may not be able to get away tonight and I have to. Call me back later and leave a message telling me when the reservations are, okay?"

"But if you're not there, will they pass the message on?"

"They will if you tell Hank I'm leaving town," Blake assured her. "Gotta go before they hog-tie her and ship her off to Timbuktu or something."

Grace hung up laughing, and Blake opened the door to find Hank skulking about. The motel proprietor pretended to straighten a picture across the hall, then stuck the rag in his back pocket. "Ah, just the man I need."

"I don't have time right now," Blake said, pushing past him and walking toward the front door.

Hank followed him, just a step behind. "But I've been thinking of expanding the motel and thought you might be able to give me some advice, seeing as how you're an expert and all."

Blake didn't even slow down, but kept on walking out the door, Hank nipping at his heels the whole way. "My advice is, don't. You don't have enough customers to warrant expansion."

Hank didn't give up. "What about remodeling,

then? Maybe we can fix things up a bit, give the old gal a face-lift, you know.''

"Good idea," Blake said as he walked down the steps cut in the side of the hill. "Get some phones in the rooms."

"I will," Hank promised. "Say, could you slow down a little?"

"Nope, not right now, I'm in a hurry."

"But, I, uh, need to talk to you about something important."

"You can talk while we walk."

Blake's brisk pace had brought him almost down to the main street when Hank grabbed his arm, looking desperate. "It's about your credit card. It's no good."

Blake stopped to fix Hank with a glare. "What do you mean, no good? My credit's excellent."

Hank gulped. "It's...expired?"

If it wasn't so irritating, it would almost be funny. Blake shook Hank's hand off his arm. "I just got a replacement last week. Try again."

"We, uh, don't take that kind."

Blake shook his head in disgust then started walking again, Hank following like an unwanted shadow. "Why didn't you tell me this when I checked in?"

"I, uh, forgot."

"Well, I'll fix it when I check out this afternoon."

"Check out?" Hank's voice came out in a squeak.

"Yes, I have to fly back to Dallas, so you don't have to invent excuses to keep me away from Lana anymore."

He was gratified to see a look of dismay cross Hank's face as he stopped dead. Blake sighed in relief. Maybe now he could make it to the diner unaccosted.

No such luck. The boy from the drugstore, Josh, came running out when he saw Blake.

"Mr. Warner, Mr. Warner, I need to talk to you."

"Talk while we walk, Josh."

Josh plucked at this sleeve. "I can't do that. I—I can't leave the store for long or I'll be fired."

Blake sighed and stopped. That was probably the truth. He might be doing the boy a disservice by assuming he was in on the conspiracy. Maybe he just wanted to talk. "Can this wait? I need to be somewhere else right now. I'll talk to you later."

"I—I just wanted to ask about that construction job in Dallas." Josh glanced down the street and Blake followed his gaze to see Ralph leaning against a streetlamp with his hands in his pockets. He whistled up at the sky while stealing peeks at the two of them.

Well, that answered Blake's question. It was another setup. He took out his card and handed it to Josh. "Call me if you get to Dallas and I'll get you a job. Gotta go now."

He strode off, but not before he caught Josh's eloquent shrug, directed at Ralph.

Blake crossed the street to try to outpace Ralph, but the little man gave up his pretense and sprinted across the street to catch up to Blake. He planted himself in Blake's path. "Mr. Warner, can I talk to you?"

Blake halted and sighed. These people never gave up. Trying to keep his irritation at bay, he said, "Not now." He moved around Ralph and continued toward the Hash House.

Ralph scurried to catch up with him. "Not now? But I think someone else is going to build a resort here—there are two strangers surveying out at Old Man Feeney's place. Feeney,'' he added in emphasis.

''It won't work, Ralph. If they're strangers, why haven't I seen them? They should be staying at the Sky Hook since it's the only motel in town.''

Ralph hurried around him to face him, walking backward. He gestured wildly. ''Only motel? Then they must be staying in Branson. That's even worse—they're hiding something from us.'' Ralph halted, bracing his hands against Blake's shoulders so he was forced to stop. ''Who do you think they are?''

Blake had to hand it to him. He had that concerned look down pat. But he wasn't buying it. Fixing Ralph with an earnest look, Blake said, ''It's all right, I know who they are.''

''You do?'' Ralph looked surprised that his stratagem had worked. ''Who are they?''

''I have it on good authority that they're aliens from Bost.'' He clapped Ralph on the arm and exerted force to move him out of the way. ''But you don't have to worry. They're only here to spy on Aunt Ona Mae.'' He continued walking, ignoring Ralph's spluttering behind him.

He made it to the diner without incident, only to find Jimmy Bartlett blocking the door.

''Morning, mayor. I'd like to go inside if you don't mind.''

Jimmy raised his beefy arm to bar the way. ''Wait. I'd like to ask you about those strangers out at the falls.''

Enough was enough. To hell with politeness— these people didn't seem to know the meaning of the word. Blake stepped forward until his chest pushed against Jimmy's arm. ''Sorry, Ralph already tried that one. And I'm fresh out of construction advice today, my credit is just fine and since I doubt you want a job in Dallas, I think you're out of stalling tactics."

The mayor's face turned red. "Stalling tactics?"

Ralph and Hank had followed Blake to the diner and they stood there, obviously wondering what to do next.

"Yes," Blake said and glared at Jimmy's arm. "I'm going inside whether you like it or not. Now, put down your arm."

Jimmy looked uncomfortable. "Now, I'm not sure I can do that, son. You'll have to make me." Then his face brightened, and he was so transparent, Blake could almost read his mind. He was obviously hoping to either make Blake look bad for tussling with a respected citizen or hoping to pin an assault charge on him.

"Yeah," Ralph the Echo said, "make him."

Before Blake could do anything, the door opened and a small, plump woman glared up at the mayor. "Don't be such a fool, Jimmy Bartlett. You let that man in and do it now."

"But, Tommie Nell," Jimmy protested.

She sniffed. "You'll do it or there won't be any chicken and dumplings for supper tonight." She leaned closer and frowned at him. "Nor any dessert neither, if you catch my meaning."

Blake stifled a laugh as Jimmy lowered his arm. Blake was wrong. The whole town wasn't against him—just the men. It seemed the women were on his side. He smiled down at Tommie Nell and said, "Thank you. Can you tell me where Lana is?"

She pointed toward the back of the diner. "There she is, but you'd better hurry."

Blake pushed past Jimmy and scanned the crowded restaurant until he spotted two men urging Lana out the back door.

One man said, "Better hurry or you'll miss the comet."

"What comet?" Lana asked, bemused. "And why do I have to go out the back way?"

Ned rose from a nearby booth. "Why don't you let her finish her lunch?"

The three men outside crowded in behind Blake. Before they could do anything else, Blake raised his voice. "Because that way she won't see me."

She and the two men turned to see who had spoken, and Lana said, "What?"

"Never mind," one of her abductors said and grabbed Lana's arm. "She was just leaving."

"She was not," Blake insisted. Then to Lana, "There is no comet. They made that up so I won't talk to you."

"Is that true?" Lana glanced at both men who looked sheepish. "Well, for heaven's sake, why?"

They shrugged, then said, "It was Jimmy's idea—"

"It figures," Hazel said. "You boys should just mind your own business."

"Me?" Jimmy protested. "What about *you?*" The diner erupted with shouts and arguments. The only ones not yelling were Blake and Lana. She stared at him with a bemused look and shrugged. Blake tried to make his way toward her, but was impeded by bickering couples all around the room.

Suddenly a shrill blast echoed through the diner. Everyone fell silent and Ned lowered the whistle from his lips. "That's better. I think I know what this is about, and I won't have it.'' He glared around at them until all the murmuring fell silent. ''Who Lana chooses is up to her, and you shouldn't interfere.''

Jimmy pointed a finger at him. ''But—''

''No buts,'' Ned insisted. ''Now, Blake, I take it you wanted to speak to Lana?''

''Yes,'' Blake answered grimly.

Ned turned to Hazel. ''Can they use your storage room?''

Hazel grinned. ''You betcha.'' She hurried to a side door. ''Right this way.''

Blake and Lana headed toward the door. As they passed, Ned stood in front of it with his arms folded, blocking everyone else's way. Tall and broad, he made a damned good barrier. Ned glared at the crowd. ''Anyone who wants to interfere will have to go through me.''

Blake paused to glance up at Ned. In a soft voice only the big man could hear, Blake asked, ''Why are you doing this? I thought you wanted her yourself.''

''I do, but I want to win her fair and square. And I want what's best for Lana. If that's you, that's fine with me.''

Blake nodded and clapped Ned on the shoulder. This is the type of man he'd be proud to call his friend. ''Thanks. And if she chooses you, I hope I'll be as gracious.''

Blake followed Hazel to the back room. Ned's simple nobility made him feel foolish, and he was beginning to wonder if he was really the best person for Lana. Was he wrong in trying to convince Lana to marry him? Would it be better for her to marry Ned? Maybe, but he wouldn't give up on her yet. He could make it work—he knew he could.

Hazel closed the door on them with a triumphant smile and, embarrassed by her neighbors' behavior, Lana looked around the tiny room. It was filled with metal shelves stacked with large-size quantities of food and strong-smelling cleaning products.

She sighed. This was ridiculous. She couldn't believe they'd been forced to talk in a closet. She gave Blake a weak smile. "You must think the whole town is a little crazy."

"No," he protested. Then at a disbelieving look from her, "Well, one or two may be a little psychotic." He smiled. "No big deal. They're doing it because they care about you."

Lana's mouth twisted in a grimace. "I wish that were true." She suspected all they really cared about was the legend.

"I think it is. They care enough about you to ensure you don't marry just anyone. At least they seem to have narrowed it down to Ned or me. It's not like they're trying to convince you to marry Jimmy or Ralph."

Lana shuddered. "No, thank heavens, but I think some of the women would rather have you for themselves."

Blake's mouth widened into a slow, sexy smile that sent her pulse pounding. He stepped closer and fingered a lock of her hair. The room temperature suddenly rose and she felt herself sway toward him.

"What about you, Lana? Would you like me for yourself?"

Yes! She realized at that moment just how much she did want him, but she wouldn't jeopardize his happiness and their baby's just to fulfill her own selfish desires. Not knowing what to say, she stared at him in confusion as he moved even closer, his gaze fixed on her mouth. "Blake, I—"

He silenced her with his lips as he cradled her head in his strong hands and kissed her, searching, demanding, needing. She couldn't help but respond, and her hormones surged as her emotions tumbled out of control.

And just like that, her body was warm and willing, ready for him. She pressed herself as close as she could get, then whimpered when she crushed her breasts against his hard chest.

He pulled away. "What's wrong?"

"I'm a lot more sensitive right now."

He touched the tip of her breast. "You mean here?"

The yearning crest hardened and she groaned with the pleasure-pain of it. "Yes, there...and elsewhere."

"You mean..."

She held her breath as he skimmed his hand down her torso until it came to rest on the hard little mound of her belly. He paused there for a moment then continued his exploration until his hand came to rest against her femininity through the thin fabric of her dress.

"...here?" he asked.

"Yes," she breathed. Ever since she'd become pregnant with his baby, she'd been in a state of semi-arousal. And now, with his simple touch, there was no "semi" about it. She was definitely aroused and wanted him to continue his explorations.

He nibbled her neck as he continued his erotic massage. Desire flowed thick and hot through her and she wanted nothing more than to pull up her dress, yank down her panties and have his probing fingers on her damp flesh. She inhaled to gain some semblance of control, and the sharp smell of disinfectant reached her.

Memory of her surroundings brought her back to awareness and she realized he had her pressed up against Hazel's storeroom door and they were making out like two teenagers. Good Lord, what was she thinking? Reluctantly, she placed her hands against his chest. "I don't think this is the right time for this…and certainly not the right place."

He nodded and removed his hands from her body but placed them on either side of her against the door. Though he was no longer touching her, she still felt protected within his embrace.

"I'm sorry," he murmured, dropping a kiss on her jaw. "It's just that I can't get you out of my mind." He cupped her neck and used his thumb to stroke her collarbone in slow, sensuous circles. "I've been thinking about you for days, but I haven't been able to get near you."

Though her nerve endings screamed for attention, Lana ignored them, trying to concentrate on his words. It was difficult. Every stroke of his thumb sent carnal pleasure skittering along her nerves, reminding her what making love with him was like. It didn't help that she could feel the full force of his desire as he pressed his hard length against her thigh.

She tried to ignore the sensations oozing through her veins and said, "It's the town's fault." His touch was making it hard to concentrate on anything so mundane as speech, but she tried anyway. "The, uh, legend."

His hand stilled. "The legend? So that's why…" He shook his head ruefully. "I should have realized."

Without the distraction of his caressing hand, Lana found the strength to slip out of his reach. Though every nerve ending in her body yearned toward him, she said, "I don't think this is why they let us come in here."

He gave her a rueful glance. "You're right." He glanced around. "It seems we're destined to discuss important decisions in closets."

"Decisions?" Fear stabbed through her. So he had another reason for seeking her out other than this desire they didn't seem to be able to control.

"Your decision," he reminded her. "Have you made one yet?"

She hesitated, feeling at this moment that she couldn't choose Ned no matter how nice he was. He never made her feel like *this*. No, it had to be Blake or nothing. But that was a tough call. "I probably won't marry Ned." Before he could say anything else, she hurried on. "But that doesn't mean I'll choose you. I still might decide to remain single."

A flash of disappointment crossed his face, then disappeared. He turned away from her, rubbing the back of his neck. "I'm sorry to hear that. I—I'd hoped we'd have more time together."

"More time?" Dread filled her. What did this mean?

"Yes, I have to cut my trip short. An emergency has come up at the office and I have to go back this afternoon."

"Oh." She should've remembered he had a life and a job back in Dallas and wouldn't be able to stay here forever. So he was giving up, just like that? She knew it was irrational, but she wanted him to stay regardless of her decision. "Are you...coming back?"

He shrugged, but avoided her eyes. "I don't know. I was lucky to get this much time away. I'm not sure if I'll be able to take any more time off for a while."

He turned toward her and she froze, sensing what came next was going to be important.

"Lana...come with me."

Stunned, she repeated, "Go with you?" It wasn't what she'd expected at all. Knowing it was foolish to hope, she nevertheless blurted out, "Why?"

His brow creased in a frown. "You have to ask? We'll never be alone here so long as the men think there's a chance you might still marry Ned."

"We don't have to be alone. We'll be able to talk on the phone." She wanted him to say that wasn't enough. She wanted to know he wanted her, needed her.

"I—I just thought you might like to see Dallas."

"Why?" she demanded, trying to force him to articulate his feelings.

He shrugged. "Wouldn't you like to get to know the city you'll be living in?"

She rebelled at the assumption she was going to wed him. "I haven't agreed yet." And she wouldn't unless she was certain it was the right thing to do. Why should she leave her family and the town she'd lived in all her life to marry someone who didn't even love her?

"I know you haven't," he said in a soothing tone. "But I'll miss you. Please come with me?"

She had a bad feeling about this. If his work was the most important thing to him now, what would happen when their baby came and he was reminded constantly of what he'd given up and why? Would he hate her then? She didn't think she could bear to raise her baby so far from home in an environment anything less than loving.

"No," she said quietly. "I don't think it's a good idea." Better to make the break now. If he loved her and really missed her, he'd come to realize it soon enough.

His shoulders slumped and she could tell he was disappointed, but all he said was, "I'm sorry to hear that. I'd really like you there." He pulled out his wallet. "Here's my card. I've asked my assistant, Grace, to book a round-trip ticket to Dallas in your name. I'll have her send you the details. If you change your mind, you're welcome anytime."

She took the card, wishing this didn't feel like goodbye. "All right, I will."

Blake gave her a half smile. "Hell, I hate leaving and giving the men just what they want. Maybe I should take Ned with me just to even the playing field."

She smiled at him. "You don't need to do that."

"I know. But if I can't have you, I might as well take *someone* with me."

But you can have me any time you want, Lana cried out silently. *All you have to do is love me.*

Chapter Nine

"Phone call for you, Blake," Grace said, appearing in the doorway of his office with a smile.

That smile could only mean one thing. "Another Bachelor Falls resident?" Someone, probably Josh or Hank, had apparently passed out his phone number to the entire town. At least, it seemed every resident had called here at least once in the past week.

She nodded. "You want me to tell her you're not in?"

Blake ran an impatient hand through his hair. "No, that's okay. They'll just keep calling and bugging you instead of me. Why don't you just transfer the calls to my phone so you won't be bothered?"

"Oh, it's no bother. Besides, I kind of like talking to these people. They have such a unique slant on life."

"I know what you mean." It was a nice change from dealing with his irascible father all day. Even though he was supposed to be retired, he was always at the office, hounding all the engineers with unreasonable demands and nitpicky details. It was beginning to drive Blake nuts, not to mention what it was doing to the staff's productivity. But, until he won the bid, his father still held controlling interest and Blake couldn't very well kick the man out of his own company.

He glanced up at Grace, who was still smiling at him. "Go ahead, send the call in."

She paused. "You know what I think?"

"What?"

"I think you like playing Blake the Builder Buddy."

He shrugged. "I don't mind. At least they appreciate it."

"And your father doesn't." It wasn't a question, it was a statement. "I think you like this hands-on stuff. Staying aloof and playing the CEO has never been your thing."

Taken aback, Blake said, "You make me sound like my father."

"No, you know when to back off and let the staff alone, and you do it. You don't like it, but you do it. Your father was never able to learn that."

"Thanks—I think."

"You're welcome." She paused, a concerned look on her face. "Blake, are you sure you really want this? You like to get your hands dirty and it's going to be even more difficult to do that once you own the company."

"I know." It had bothered him, too, but he wouldn't admit it. "But then the stress level will be lower because I won't have anyone second-guessing me."

"You won't?" she asked with a raised eyebrow.

"Lord, I hope not." He glanced at the phone. "Better send that call in. Who is it?"

"I didn't quite catch her name. Something... Mae?"

"Oh, yes, Aunt Ona Mae."

"Aunt?"

He waved a hand in embarrassment. "Oh, everyone calls her aunt—it's sort of an honor."

Grace grinned at him again. "One of these days, I'm gonna have to visit this town you're so attached to."

Attached? Ridiculous. "No, it's just that they need my help so much. And they're grateful for it." Unlike his father.

"Yeah, right. Well, if you ask me, I think you're falling in love with the town. I'll just send *Aunt* Ona Mae on in."

Before he could reply to that shot, she'd left and soon the phone was buzzing.

"Blake?" Auntie Om said in a querulous tone.

"Yes, how can I help you?" He sat back, prepared to enjoy whatever problem the amusing woman had come up with.

"I'm a little worried about them Bostians," she said in a penetrating tone. He hadn't been able to convince her that, even though he was in a different state, she didn't need to shout to be heard. Instead, he'd learned to hold the receiver far from his ear.

"Why is that?"

"I've tried and tried to get a look at those two strangers, but everyone has seen them but me," she complained. "If I could just get close to one, I could tell right off if they're from Bost or not. I just know they've come to take me away, but no one believes me."

"It's all right," Blake soothed. "Maybe they're not Bostians. They might just be two men on vacation."

"Not with them strange tools I hear tell they're using, they're not."

"Well, even if they are from Bost, they're probably avoiding you because...because you're the only one who could reveal them for what they really are." He paused. "You don't have anything to worry about. They wouldn't dare reveal themselves to anyone but you. Just make sure you're never alone when you go out of the house, and you won't have anything to worry about." He'd probably just condemned the whole town to waiting on Auntie Om, but they did that already anyway.

There was silence on the other end for a moment, then she said, "All right. I'll just make sure them sorry polecats never catch *me* alone."

"Good—"

"Wait. Someone else wants to talk to you."

Blake sighed in resignation, hoping the whole town wasn't lined up waiting to talk.

"Blake?" came a softer voice. "This is Serena Talbot, Lana's mother."

"How are you, Mrs. Talbot?" Blake asked politely, wondering why she wanted to speak to him.

"Fine. I just wondered...are you coming back soon?"

He sighed. "I don't know. Unfortunately, my job is keeping me very busy right now. I'd like to return after I straighten out this problem but...I don't know if Lana wants me to."

"Of course she does. Why, she talks about you all the time."

Knowing it was wishful thinking and more than

likely a kind fib, Blake said, "But she still hasn't agreed to marry me."

"I know, but if you're not here, Ned is going to steal a march on you. Why, he's been at her house almost every day."

Now *that* he didn't know—Lana hadn't mentioned it in their daily telephone conversations. "She told me she wasn't going to marry Ned." Who was he reminding? Serena or himself?

"She's not?" Serena asked with a note of surprise and gladness in her voice. "But if she doesn't marry you or Ned, what's going to happen to her job? The old coot Jimmy Bartlett is serious about firing her."

"I don't know. I can't force her, Mrs. Talbot."

"I know," she said in exasperation. "No one could ever force that child to do anything. But if you're not here, how can you talk her into it?"

It was rotten of him, but he couldn't help saying, "She could come here. I invited her to Dallas and even gave her a ticket."

"You did? Why, that little scamp! She never told me. Well, I'll have a thing or two to tell her."

Feeling guilty at setting Lana's mother on her, Blake said, "Wait. Don't say anything yet. Let me call her and ask her again. If she refuses, then you can be the second team and do your part to eradicate the legend from Bachelor Falls."

"All right, that sounds fair enough." She paused. "But I'll have you know the legend isn't the only reason I'm doing this. I care about my daughter and I believe you are the best thing for her—even if she doesn't know her own mind yet."

Flattered, Blake said, "Thank you, but...you don't really know me. How can you say that?"

"Well, I know you did the right thing in offering to marry her. And I know you've been helping folks hereabouts with building things...and you've been nice to Ona Mae when you didn't have to. That sounds like the kind of man I'd like for a son-in-law."

Blake didn't know what to say, and Serena added, "Besides, I figure you and she have more feelings for each other than you let on." Before he could react to that outrageous remark, she went on. "That reminds me—Ona Mae was right. There *are* two men sniffing up by Old Man Feeney's place."

"The aliens?"

"No," she answered with a laugh. "But they don't show their faces in town. I'm afraid they're up to no good."

"What do you expect me to do about it?"

"I don't know what you can do, but the mayor seems to think you might know how to handle 'em."

"Then why doesn't he call me?"

Exasperated, Serena said, "Because he's afraid you'd come back to Bachelor Falls and he'd have to marry Tommie Nell."

Strangely enough, Blake followed that logic. "Well, I don't want to butt in where I'm not wanted. And I'm not sure I could help anyway."

He couldn't blame the guys for wanting to avoid the nosy citizens of Bachelor Falls. They were probably just up there fishing, where Blake wished he could be right now. "But if Mayor Bartlett wants my advice, he'll have to call me himself."

Serena sighed. "Okay. When are you going to call Lana?"

"Right now," he promised. Before Serena could pester her so much she didn't want to come.

They said their goodbyes, and he got up to close the door. Grace was outside talking to his secretary and raised an eyebrow at him. "Going to call Lana?" She glanced at her watch. "A little early, isn't it?"

He scowled at her and shut the door without answering. She was too knowing for his taste. He didn't think he'd been so obvious, but the closed door probably gave him away.

With anticipation, he dialed Lana's number. He'd limited himself to one call a day, usually in late afternoon when there was a lull in the activity here. He'd thought about calling her from home, but didn't want to do it from bed where all sorts of images kept popping up.

He dialed Lana's number and smiled when she answered the phone with a voice that seemed to caress the airwaves.

"Hi," he said simply, and leaned back in his chair to relax. "It's me."

"Hello, you," she teased. "It's a little early for your call."

"That's what Grace said," he complained. "Am I that predictable?"

"Oh, just a little. I'll bet you have me penciled in your calendar—'call Lana at five p.m.'"

He scowled. Another woman who thought she had him pegged. All right, so it was on his calendar. So what? It was only so his secretary didn't schedule him for any meetings or appointments at that time. But he understood the subtext of her comment. "Calling you isn't a chore or a duty," he protested. "It's the high spot of my day."

"Mine, too," she answered softly.

"So, tell me about your day."

She babbled on about the schoolchildren and catalog shopping for maternity clothes and baby furniture. Blake didn't listen too closely. All he noticed was what she'd left out. When she paused, he said, "I hear Ned has been visiting you every day."

Damn—he hadn't meant to blurt it out like that and sound like a jealous teenager. Who she saw was her business.

"Yes, he stops by every morning to check on me. Why?"

Her voice was flat, and Blake hurried to say, "No reason. I'm just surprised you hadn't mentioned it before. Have you...changed your mind about him?"

Her voice softened. "No, I haven't changed my mind. In fact, I told him I wasn't going to marry him." She hurried to add, "But that doesn't mean I'm going to marry anyone else either. Ned just stops by to keep the mayor off his back and mine. Only the three of us know that, though."

"Uh, make that four. Your mother called this morning and kind of mentioned it."

Lana sighed. "So that's what prompted this early call. I'm sorry she called you. I'll tell her to leave you alone."

"That's okay. She's your mother—she has a right to know what my plans are with respect to you. Besides, I'm afraid I sicced her on you."

"How?"

"By telling her I invited you to Dallas."

"Gee, thanks," Lana said. "Now she'll never leave me alone."

"You wouldn't have to worry about it if you came to visit me. Wouldn't it be nice to get away from the harassment for a few days?" he wheedled.

"Well, I do have spring break next week, but what will I do while you're working?"

"I have to work tomorrow, but I plan on taking the weekend off, all but a few hours. And I'd like you to see where I live."

"I don't know—"

"There's great shopping here in Dallas," he reminded her. "You'll have a lot better selection of maternity clothes and baby stuff."

"You don't really want to spend your free weekend shopping, do you?"

Sensing she was weakening, he said, "It's the least a knight could do for his damsel." He paused and lowered his voice. "Besides, I've been missing out on most of your pregnancy and the growth of our baby. I'd like to participate in some way." He was manipulating her, true, but it was the truth just the same.

"Oh, Blake, I didn't think. I'd love to shop for baby stuff with you."

"Then you'll come?"

"Yes. Let me call the airline to see if they have a flight tomorrow afternoon."

"Good—just call and let me know when it's coming in. I'll meet you or make sure someone else does. And, Lana?"

"Yes?"

"I'm looking forward to seeing you again."

"So am I," she whispered.

They said their goodbyes and hung up, then Blake put his hands behind his head, smiling at the ceiling.

The door opened and Grace stuck her head in. "I saw the light go off on your phone. So, what's up?"

"What makes you think something's up?"

"Well, let's see. You get a phone call from Bachelor Falls then call Lana hours before your scheduled time. There's gotta be something up."

"Lord, you're nosy."

"Yep, deal with it. Come on, give."

"If you must know...Lana's coming out tomorrow to visit for the weekend."

Grace's smile broadened. "Good. I've been wanting to meet the woman who could put that look on your face." She sauntered away before Blake could answer.

He scowled. *What look?*

AS THE PLANE LANDED in Dallas, Lana remembered the last time she'd flown. That trip had complicated her life tremendously. She wondered if this one would prove to be as life shattering.

It might. She planned to use the time here to decide whether or not to marry Blake. But first, she needed to know if he'd changed. When he'd left Bachelor Falls, she'd gotten the impression he wanted to marry her only out of duty, but his daily phone calls belied that.

Since he'd been away she'd seen a different side of him. He seemed genuinely interested in her and what she was doing, and their conversations had been long and newsy as they'd gotten to know each other better. Much like that magical flight to Las Vegas where they'd connected like two lost souls.

Was he coming to care for her as much as she did for him, or was it an illusion fostered by the false intimacy of the phone calls? She had to know.

Not because her job depended on it—no matter what she did, she'd no longer be teaching school in

Bachelor Falls. If she married Blake, he wanted her to live with him in Dallas. If she didn't marry him, she wouldn't marry anyone and the school board wouldn't let her return to work after the summer.

No, her job wasn't the issue, but her baby was. She could find work, but finding her baby a set of parents who loved each other would be more difficult.

She spared a moment to worry, but shunted it aside. First things first. She had to make the decision this weekend, then she'd think about a job. Despite the fact that Purple Bunny was still missing, she hoped everything would work out. It had to.

She disembarked from the plane and looked around for Blake, but didn't see him. A woman approached Lana with a smile. "Hi, you must be Lana. I'd know you anywhere."

The diminutive, sophisticated woman in the red power suit held out her hand. Feeling like a hick in her pink flowered dress, Lana shook the offered hand. "Yes, I'm Lana Talbot. But, how do you know me?"

"I'm Grace Warner," the woman said. "Blake's cousin and assistant. He asked me to meet you and described you to a *T.*"

"Oh." Lana tried to hide her disappointment by giving Grace a smile. "I remember talking to you on the phone."

She must not have been very successful in concealing her chagrin because Grace squeezed her hand. "He wanted to meet you, but he had to attend an emergency meeting." Her mouth twisted in a grimace. "Damage control—his father managed to get hold of the Palladian bid and screw it up."

At Lana's blank look, Grace said, "Never mind.

Take my word for it, he had to go though he didn't want to."

Reassured by Grace's friendliness, Lana followed her to the baggage claim area and out to the car where she stroked the soft leather of the car seat, unused to such luxury.

Once they were on the freeway, Grace gave her a sidelong glance. "I'm glad Blake couldn't make it—I wanted to meet you."

"You did?" What possible interest could this elegant woman have in her?

"Yes, I wanted to meet the woman who could throw Blake for a loop."

"Me?" Lana squeaked, unable to believe her ears. She was the one who'd been thrown for a loop.

Grace grinned. "Yes, you. I've never seen him so distracted. He's positively unfocused. What magic did you use? I'd like to make a man feel that way about me."

Flabbergasted, Lana could do nothing but stare. Blake had never shown that sort of interest in her. "That's kind of you," she managed to say, "but I didn't do anything. I'm just a schoolteacher." She gestured at Grace's sophisticated perfection and her own simple dress, inviting her to see the contrast.

"That's your secret then—you're just naturally sweet and unassuming, not to mention gorgeous." Grace heaved a dramatic sigh. "I just wish I was tall, blond and voluptuous, too."

"But, isn't Blake used to women a little more...worldly?"

"He used to be—and that's probably why you made such an impression. So, when are you going to say yes and put him out of his misery?"

A little taken aback at Grace's sudden change of subject, Lana didn't know what to say.

"He's told me everything, you know." Grace gave a significant glance at Lana's waistline.

The floaty dress Lana wore disguised her pregnancy, so Blake must have mentioned it. Rather liking this woman who was so professional yet so personable, Lana said, "I'm going to make a decision this weekend."

"Good. You couldn't find a better guy."

"I know."

"So why are you keeping him hanging?" She said it in a light tone, but Lana heard the steel underneath.

Raising an eyebrow, Lana said, "You don't pull any punches, do you?"

"Not when it comes to people I care about. Blake is not only my cousin and my boss, he's my friend, too."

Lana nodded. "I have friends like that." She'd react the same if it were Ellie or Kelly on the line.

"Then you understand when I say I want him to be happy. He's had a hard life with carrying the heavy responsibility of his family on his back. He needs someone to love him for himself."

Lana decided to lay it on the line. "I do, too," she said softly. "And so does our baby."

Grace's eyebrows rose. "You think he won't?"

"I don't know—that's what I'm here to find out. Call me foolish, but I want my baby to grow up in a loving atmosphere, not one dictated by duty."

"Even if you lose your teaching job?"

Blake really had told her everything. "Yes," she said simply. Somehow, she knew everything would work out. It had to.

"Then I wouldn't call you foolish—I'd call you brave."

Lana shrugged. She didn't see it that way. She was just doing what she had to in order to get the best life for her baby.

Grace pulled into an apartment complex, saying, "Well, here we are."

"Where's here?"

"Blake's apartment. We just assumed you'd be staying with him?" It was more of a question than a statement.

Lana hadn't thought about it, but supposed it made sense. She just hoped the town wouldn't hear about it—they'd be scandalized. "This will be fine," Lana said. She'd see more of Blake this way—between meetings anyway.

Grace led the way through the posh lobby and up the elevator to Blake's apartment. Once inside, Lana glanced around with trepidation. Decorated in stark black and white with splashes of bloodred, the living room was very cold...and vastly different from her own homey abode. Blake lived here? How could he stand it?

Her expression must have mirrored her feelings, for Grace said, "Blake hired one of our cousins to do the decorating, and she went a little overboard with the dramatic look. Don't worry—I'm sure he'll let you change it."

Lana merely nodded. She'd have to.

"Come on," Grace said. "I'll show you to your room." She opened the door to a room that wasn't quite so dramatic, though the bright yellows and greens were a bit much. "Blake's room is across the hall."

Lana was relieved she wouldn't have the added pressure of sleeping in the same bed. This way, they could ease into whatever relationship they decided on.

Once she'd deposited her things in the bedroom, Grace led her into a kitchen full of shiny metal appliances and set her down with a cup of herbal tea. They whiled away the time by discussing Blake's childhood. A picture emerged of a bright, enthusiastic young man who'd been thrust into responsibility when an accident had left the Warner Construction Company with one of its partners dead and the other severely injured.

His uncle, Grace's father, had been the business head while Blake's father had overseen the construction. With his partner dead and himself injured, Blake's father had needed someone else to oversee the administrative side of the company, so he'd taken Blake into the family business. Not only was he the oldest of all the cousins, but he had a degree in business and knew company operations since he'd worked there for several summers. Because of that, his father had trained him to be the CEO. But even though his father was injured and supposedly retired, he couldn't keep his hands out of the business.

Lana soaked up all the information she could, wanting to understand what made Blake tick.

When he walked into the kitchen a couple of hours later, Lana stood and wiped her damp palms on her dress. He looked so imposing and important in his suit, making her feel out of place and nervous. She was in his world now and didn't know how to react.

Blake smiled and took a step toward her, then flicked a glance at Grace and faltered. "I'm glad you could make it," he said awkwardly.

"So am I."

Grace rolled her eyes. "Jeez, you guys. Forget I'm here, Blake, and kiss the woman."

Blake grinned and moved toward Lana. "Whatever you say."

He gathered Lana into his arms and kissed her...a warm, soft, inviting kiss that made her feel at home. She smiled up into his eyes and sighed when he released her lips. Sheer heaven. But was that the kiss of a man in love?

"Well," Grace said. "Now that you're home, I'll leave. That is, if you're not taking off again."

"I'm not," Blake said. "Thanks for taking care of her."

"No problem. Treat her right, cousin. I want this one in the family."

Startled and pleased by Grace's unexpected championing, Lana gave her an impulsive hug. But once Grace left, she and Blake were alone with awkwardness still between them.

Blake gestured her toward the white sofa and he took the black. "So," Lana said, "how was your meeting?" She could have kicked herself for uttering such a mundane question.

He grimaced. "Don't ask. Look, I'm sorry I had to leave you on your own so long. I didn't intend—"

"It's okay," she interrupted. "I didn't expect you to change your entire routine for me."

He rubbed the back of his neck. "Well, I did. And that's not the worst of it."

"You have to go back to work?" she asked, trying to hide her disappointment.

"No, but I cut this meeting short and told my father why. He wants to meet you."

He said it with such trepidation that Lana couldn't help but feel some herself. "Why? Does he know about…our situation?"

"No, I only told Grace. But I had to explain why I needed to leave the meeting, and when he heard a woman friend was flying in to spend the weekend, he insisted we have dinner with him and Mom tonight."

An inspection? She gulped. "I—I'd love to meet your parents." She'd have to sooner or later anyway, if she married him. Might as well get it over with now.

His look of relief was worth the little white lie. He glanced at his watch. "Thank you. I won't mention…anything else until you're ready. We're meeting them in an hour."

"Then I'd better get ready."

"Why? You look fine to me."

Just like a man. "Thank you, but I just want to shed some of the grime of travel and put on something that isn't quite so wrinkled."

"Okay, thanks for being such a sport."

She showered and changed into a dress she'd brought along for just such an occasion. Pretty and feminine, it was constructed in soft green and blue pastel-washed silk that cascaded in layers from her chest down to her knees and concealed her pregnancy. She slipped on some simple pumps, a small gold chain and earrings, dabbed on some makeup and was ready.

As she entered the living room, the pleasure on Blake's face was her reward. He smiled and kissed her cheek. "You look so beautiful, I think I'd rather stay home tonight and keep you for myself."

Her heart leapt in anticipation as she stared into his

eyes, only inches from her own. "That's fine with me."

His gaze lingered on her lips then moved to the soft swell of her breasts for a moment, but he shook his head. "No, we'd better go or I'll never hear the end of it."

Not knowing whether to be pleased or annoyed, Lana merely nodded and followed him out the door.

The restaurant was definitely upscale. Hushed conversations of elegantly dressed people filled the room, and there were so many diamonds and so much crystal that the atmosphere positively sparkled. Lana felt a bit out of place, but was very glad she'd changed for dinner so she could at least hold her own.

Blake's parents were already there, and Lana gulped as she followed him to their table, hoping she would be able to love them...or at least *like* them if they were to be her baby's grandparents.

Her heart sank when she saw them for the first time. They didn't look like the type of folks who would consider a simple schoolteacher to be a proper wife for their son. Blake's mother, sleek and smart in her navy evening suit and pearls, gave Lana a rather disdainful look, and his gruff father apologized for not standing. Since he was in a wheelchair, she hadn't expected him to, but he seemed annoyed with her for some reason.

Lana smiled as Blake seated her, wishing she had the courage to run out the door. It was the old "fight or flight" syndrome, but she didn't want to do either. She forced her apprehension down, hoping things wouldn't be as bad as they appeared at first sight.

They were worse.

Mrs. Warner gave her an insincere smile. "So, dear, what do you do?"

Deciding to get it over with right away, Lana said, "I teach grade school...in Missouri."

The woman's eyes glazed over. "How...nice." Then, turning away from Lana, she spoke to Blake. "You know, that reminds me. I saw Cynthia the other day and she's still modeling. She asked about you, dear. Are you going to call her soon?"

Blake slanted an apologetic glance at Lana. "No, we went out a few times but we just didn't click."

"Don't be silly," Mrs. Warner purred. "Why, you would click with anyone. And Cynthia is beautiful, not to mention smart."

"I'm seeing Lana now," Blake said firmly.

Lana squirmed in her chair, wondering if it would be possible to pretend a splitting headache so she could leave.

"Humph," his father said. "What about that Hawthorne girl? Damn fine filly, if you ask me."

"Cissy Hawthorne and I aren't interested in each other either."

"Too bad. The merger of Hawthorne and Warner is just what our company needs."

Lana saw Blake's jaw clench but he said in a light tone, "Then you marry her."

"Blake!" His mother's voice was shocked. "Don't talk to your father that way. You know he isn't well."

At Blake's silence, his mother continued. "Now, dear, tell me, have you investigated that investment for me?"

Over the course of the dinner, Lana watched as Blake's parents put more and more demands on him, inundating him with family responsibilities and chores. But they all seemed to take it as natural, and Lana couldn't help but pity Blake. How could he live his own life when he was so busy helping everyone else?

Luckily the Warners ignored her after the first few moments, obviously hoping she'd go away. Lana wished it, too, but felt constrained to stick by Blake. He, at least, showed good manners by trying to involve Lana in the conversation. But his parents were either too self-involved or too contemptuous of her to let him get away with it.

Finally the awful dinner was over and they were able to escape, but not before Blake's father insisted Blake come to another meeting on Sunday, no matter how much he protested he wanted to be with his guest.

Once inside the car, Blake turned to her with an apologetic look. "I'm sorry. I can't believe how rude they were. I'll talk to them about it tomorrow. I promise, it won't happen again."

"Don't worry about it," she murmured. He was right. It wouldn't happen again, because she wouldn't let it. She couldn't possibly live in his stark apartment with his cold parents in this big noisy city. She shuddered at the thought of them as grandparents to her baby.

Well, there was one good thing about this evening. She now knew what her decision had to be. As soon as they got back to Blake's apartment, she'd tell him she wouldn't marry him.

Chapter Ten

Sadness filled Lana, but she knew it was the only decision she could make. She had hoped things would work out, and had even been willing to move to Dallas and leave the home she loved if she was convinced it would be the best environment for her baby. But this evening had capped the disastrous trip.

There was only one way she and her baby could live here and be happy...and that was if Blake loved them. Wishing it were true, she decided to give him one more chance.

They entered Blake's apartment and he drew her into his arms, murmuring, "Alone at last."

He lowered his head and kissed her...and Lana couldn't help but respond. She poured her heart and soul into that kiss, slanting her hungry mouth beneath his, holding him as close as possible, trying to merge their bodies, their souls.

Desperately, she willed him to feel some measure of the love she felt for him, to open up and admit it, to tell her he loved her. Desire rose hot and fierce within her, both physical and emotional. She needed him so much, on many different levels, but...did he feel the same way about her? Oh, he wanted her physically—his erection was proof of that, but was there anything else?

He raised his head from that soul-searing kiss and cupped her sensitive breasts in both hands, whispering, ''God, I missed this.''

She saw desire in his eyes, but no love. He wanted her all right, but it was more an obsession with the contours of her body than with the workings of her mind and soul. With regret, she pulled away from his caressing hands.

She missed this, too, but it was no substitute for the love she and her baby needed to live a happy life. And it wouldn't be fair to make love to Blake, no matter how much she wanted to, when she knew she planned to never see him again.

''What's wrong?'' Blake asked.

''This won't work,'' she said, turning her face away.

''I thought it was working great.'' He reached out to touch her arm. ''Is it my parents? Don't worry about them. They react that way whenever they perceive a threat.''

Lana turned to look into his eyes. ''I'm a threat?''

''They see it that way. I'm sure they sense I'm thinking about marrying you, and are afraid it will take me from them.''

It wasn't the answer she'd hoped for. ''I don't want to be a threat to anyone,'' she murmured. ''And it will be worse once they learn about the baby.''

Blake frowned. ''No, they'll love the child because it will be a Warner. That won't be a problem.''

''Maybe. But you're so involved in your family, I doubt there will be room for me and my baby.''

All desire was now gone from his face. "I won't give up my family," he said bluntly.

Their baby was his family, too. Couldn't he see that? "I'm not asking you to." All she was asking was to share a small part of that love, to have a small corner of his heart.

"My family is important, but I'll never neglect you or the child," he assured her.

He'd never love her either, she saw that now. He saw the world in black and white. She was either one of the people he was responsible for or she wasn't. She couldn't live like that. Without love, how long would it be before he began resenting her and their baby as much as he obviously resented the rest of his family for depending on him?

"Tell you what," he coaxed. "I'll blow off the meeting on Sunday and we'll go shopping for the baby all weekend, just the two of us."

Just the two of them? No, his family would always be along in spirit, pulling on him, making demands on him. She could never compete with that. "No, that's all right," she said softly. "Go to your meeting. I'm leaving tomorrow morning."

Blake stared at her in shock. "Leaving? Why?"

"Because I've made my decision." She averted her gaze, unable to look him in the eyes as she delivered the lie. "I'm going to marry Ned." It was kinder for both of them. This way Blake would no longer feel responsible for her, and she could cut all ties cleanly.

"Ned? But you said you wouldn't marry him."

She shrugged. "I changed my mind. I have to do what's best for my baby."

"You think Ned is best?" he asked in an incredulous tone.

She risked a glance at him and the hurt on his face almost caused her to change her mind. But not quite. "He loves me and will love the child as his own." She willed Blake to say that he would love her and their baby, too.

There was nothing but silence as his expression turned stony. "So," he said softly. "I'm no longer your white knight."

Lana blinked back tears. "I'm afraid not."

She'd lied again. He would be her white knight forever, but only in her heart.

BLAKE WALKED into the office, still feeling numb. Lana had left yesterday morning in a cab, refusing to even let him take her to the airport. He wanted to feel angry, betrayed or *something*, but he was devoid of emotion. The hurt was there, down deep somewhere, but it was locked up inside him and refused to let itself out.

He mumbled a distracted greeting to Grace as he walked past her into his office.

"Hey," Grace said. "What are you doing here?"

"The same thing you are. I work here, remember?"

"I just came in to do a couple of things before tomorrow. Why are you working on Sunday?"

He shrugged. "Dad called another meeting."

Grace shook her head in exasperation. "Of all times. What about Lana?"

Blake stared down at the desk, unwilling to let Grace see his feelings, even if he didn't quite know what they were. "She's gone," he said in a flat tone.

"She went shopping by herself? You should have told me. I'd have gone with her."

"No, I mean *gone*—back to Bachelor Falls."

"Already? Why?"

He'd like to know the answer to that himself. "After she met my parents, she decided to marry Ned," he said dryly. Not for the first time, rebellion rose in him. When would he be able to live his life the way *he* wanted to without interference from his family?

"But I don't understand. She loves you."

A quiver of emotion fluttered in his chest but he beat it back. Lana had made it plain there was no room for hope. "She's going to marry Ned."

Concern evident in her eyes, Grace shook her head. "That doesn't mean she loves him."

"Why else would she marry him?" There had to be a reason Blake had lost out to the other man.

Ignoring his question, Grace said, "Well, you should be glad. You wanted her out of your system and this way you get what you want, without the added burden."

Taken aback, Blake said, "I'd still always take care of my child."

"Yes, but this is the easy way—all you have to do is send money. You won't have to give up any more time."

Appalled, he wondered if he'd given Lana this impression, too. "It's not like that."

"It's not? Why?"

"Because..." He sought for a plausible reason, but knew only one thing. "Because I want to be with her."

"The sex is that good, huh? Well, you can find that with anyone else."

"No," he protested. Blake couldn't believe Grace was so callous. And the idea of making love to anyone other than Lana held no appeal. Shocked, he examined that feeling, but Grace didn't give him a chance to wonder at it.

"No? What does Lana have that other women don't?"

Compassion, a rich sensuality and curves a man could sink into. But he couldn't say that. "She has my baby."

"Ah, I see you haven't figured it out yet."

"Huh?"

"Never mind. That's not good enough."

"Why not?"

"You're a lot slower than I thought. You twit—all Lana really wants is to be loved."

"How do you know?"

"She told me so."

"She did? Well, I can't force a love I don't feel."

Grace grinned at him, raising one eyebrow. "Well, if you can't, it appears this Ned can."

That was low. "But I care for her. That's a start, and I'm sure I'll come to love her in time. And of course I'll love my child. What more can she ask?"

"You know."

Annoyed with Grace's enigmatic comments, Blake suddenly realized he did want Lana as his wife. Not because it was his obligation to do so, not because she was carrying his child, but because he wanted her for himself. "I really want to marry her," he whispered to himself in disbelief.

"Then tell her so."

"Tell her?"

"Yes. Remember when I told you to find the old you, the Blake I used to know? Well, you've been more relaxed and more happy since you met Lana than I've seen you in the past ten years." She paused, staring at him earnestly. "You need that part of you. And if Lana is the catalyst, then don't lose her. Fight for her, Blake."

Now she was making sense. "You're right." He reached for the phone.

Grace put her hand atop his. "Not that way."

"Right again." He paused as a horrible thought struck him. "But what if she won't see me? What if my parents have turned her off so much she won't marry me?"

"She will," Grace said in a confident tone. "Just search your heart and tell her how you really feel."

That he didn't love her yet, but really wanted to marry her anyway? That didn't make sense. "Tell her what?"

"That's for you to figure out. Don't worry—she'll marry you."

"I hope you're right," Blake said. "I'll call the airport right now and..."

"What's wrong?"

Disappointment filled him. "I can't. Father called a meeting today on the Palladian bid."

"Do you have to be there?"

He wished he could just skip out, but he couldn't mess this up. Not when what he had been working for all his life was so close within his grasp. But he couldn't lose Lana either. Not for the first time, he felt torn between two conflicting duties.

Then it dawned on him. No, not two—only one of them was a duty. The other was a deep-seated need to find and win Lana back. He'd sacrificed enough of his life to expedience. He wouldn't let this go, too. Without analyzing *why* he felt this need, he said,

"You take the meeting for me—and finish up the bid."

"Me?"

"Yes—you know almost as much about the project as I do. I'll just fill you in on a few things and you can take over."

"But...your father will never go for it."

Blake had run up against his father's unreasoning doubts about Grace's capability before, but he waved it aside. "That's what makes it so perfect. He won't complain about you taking over because he'll assume you'll fail. Then when we win the bid, he'll have to not only hand over the reins of the company to me, but admit you know your job, too."

Grace regarded him in awe. "I can't believe you'd put your future in my hands."

"Why not?" he asked, feeling jubilant. "I know you'll do a great job. If you can't win that bid for Warner, I can't either—no one could. And just to make sure you don't have any problems getting what you need, I'll send out a memo making you vice president."

At first she seemed speechless, then recovered. "You can do that?"

"Father and I have been talking about doing it for a long time and the paperwork is already in motion. We were just waiting until you were ready." Blake had thought her so long ago, but his father hadn't been so sure. "You're ready now."

A smile transformed her face. "Thanks, Blake. You won't regret it. I—"

The phone rang then and Grace picked it up. "Warner Construction."

Her eyebrows rose and her mouth twitched as she

handed the phone to Blake. "It's Mayor Bartlett from Bachelor Falls."

How did the man know he'd be here on a Sunday morning? "Hello," Blake said. "How can I help you, Mayor?"

"It's those two men," Jimmy growled without preamble. Blake could picture him stabbing the air with a cigar. "You gotta do something about them."

"What two men?" What was this, a mass delusion?

"Those two who've been surveying out at Old Man Feeney's place. They're from Warner Construction."

That got Blake's attention. "From here? Are you sure?" How could that be? He hadn't sent anyone there.

"That's what their equipment says. And they've done bought the land already." The mayor's voice turned suspicious. "What's going on, Warner? You told us you weren't building a resort."

"I'm *not*. But I'll check on it right away, I promise you that."

"Good. See that you do."

Jimmy hung up and Blake turned to stare at Grace. "He said two men from Warner just bought land out by the falls and are surveying it."

Grace looked skeptical. "Maybe he's just using that as an excuse to get you back."

Blake rejected that idea. "No—he doesn't want me there. He wants Lana to marry Ned."

She looked thoughtful. "Then ask the head of our real-estate section. He'll know if we've bought any land there." She picked up the phone. "I'll call him at home."

"No, that's all right. You should be getting ready

for the meeting.'' Blake handed her the contents of his briefcase. ''Start boning up on the Palladian bid and I'll make the call.''

Fifteen minutes later, he hung up the phone and stared off into space.

''What's wrong?'' Grace asked. ''What did you find out?''

''We did put in a bid on the land,'' he muttered. ''The real-estate section thought they were doing it under my orders, because Dad told them to.''

''But why in Bachelor Falls? I don't understand.''

''I don't know, but I'm going to find out.'' Whatever the reason, it couldn't be a good one. ''I'll check it out as soon as I get there tomorrow.''

Why would his father want to build a resort there and keep it a secret? Not only would it be bad for the town, but bad for the company, too—it was too far from ready transportation and other amenities to be profitable.

Whatever the reason, it was good to have a positive plan of action again. All he needed to do was go to Bachelor Falls, convince Lana to marry him, investigate these surveyors and save the town.

He grinned. The white knight was back in action again.

Chapter Eleven

Lana watched from the lunch counter as Hazel served customers and waited for a free moment. She shouldn't feel nervous. She'd known Hazel all her life, but this was different. This time she'd come to ask for a job.

As soon as she'd gotten home from Dallas and had time to think, Lana had realized that, as a consequence of her decision to remain single, she was going to have to find a new position somewhere. Unfortunately, she didn't think she'd enjoy anything as much as she did teaching, but the mayor was stubborn. He wouldn't back down in his pronouncement that she had to be married or she'd lose her job at the end of this school year.

Though her mother had offered to support Lana and the baby, Lana didn't want to be dependent on anyone. She needed to make her own way in life. That meant she had to find another job.

The only problem was, everyone knew her circumstances and she'd been turned down by five local businesses already. Not because she was unqualified, but because they knew she was pregnant and wanted her to choose a husband, urging her to wed either

Blake or Ned, depending on which side of the controversy they championed.

Stubborn fools. What if she didn't marry and couldn't find a job when the baby came? Surely someone would relent and give her one...but she couldn't count on it, and didn't want them to do so just because they felt sorry for her. She was a hard worker and would do anything that wouldn't hurt her baby.

Lana had high hopes for a job with Hazel. It looked as though she needed help and she sure wouldn't let the dictates of the mayor decree who she could and couldn't hire.

Hazel finished with her other customers and swiped the counter in front of Lana. "Hi, hon. What'll it be?"

"I need a job," Lana blurted out. No sense beating around the bush. Before Hazel's uncertain expression could settle into negativity, Lana hurried on. "You look like you could use another waitress. You know I'd do a good job, and I'd work any hours you want, give you a break." She paused for breath, then said, "How about it? Will you hire me?"

Hazel gave her a pitying look. "Now, hon, you don't want to work here."

Given a choice, no, but it didn't look as though she had one. "Sure I do."

"No, you don't. It's tough work for anyone, on your feet all day and all. You're not used to it. Why, it'd kill your back, and with the baby coming, it would just make things worse."

Had Hazel joined the Pregnancy Police, too? "I can handle it," Lana said stubbornly. "And I really need this job. Please, Hazel?"

The older woman sighed. "I'm sorry, sugar, but I'm gonna have to say no. I can't afford to hire anyone else. If you really needed to work, I might take you on, but the plain fact is, you don't. You got two nice men just dying to hitch up with you. Why are you being so stubborn? Why don't you just marry one of them, for heaven's sake?"

Lana was beginning to wonder about that herself. Was her stubbornness and insistence on love going to hurt her baby? That was the last thing she wanted.

She opened her mouth to try a different tack, but Hazel's gaze strayed to the window. "What the heck is going on out there?"

Lana turned to look. The crowd outside seemed excited about something. Her curiosity roused, she opened the door and glanced out. They seemed to be tussling over something in their midst. What an odd sight. She would have expected it of teenagers, but most of these folks were her mother's age.

Dressed in their Sunday best, men formed a ring on the inside with women on the outside beating on their backs with fists and flailing purses. No one was throwing punches yet, but she could tell it was only a matter of time. As Lana watched in disbelief, Aunt Ona Mae bopped Ralph on the head with her shoe.

He winced and glanced over his shoulder, then yelled, "Uh-oh. Lana's here."

Everyone turned to look at her. Even more curious now, Lana said, "What's going on?"

Tommie Nell, who had Jimmy Bartlett in a half nelson, cried out, "It's Blake. The men won't let him see you."

Hope flashed through Lana but she quelled it. Just

because Blake was back didn't mean he'd come to declare his undying love.

"Stop this," Lana yelled. "Stop it now."

They paid no attention to her and kept on scuffling. She couldn't even see Blake, who she supposed was in the middle of the ruckus. Lana glanced around for something to stop them and saw Ned drive up in his pickup. He had to slow down when he reached the crowd because it was blocking the entire street. Rolling down his window, he called out to Lana, "What's going on?"

She ran over and pointed to the melee. "Blake's in the middle of that. They're trying to stop him from talking to me. Can you do something?"

Ned shook his head in disbelief, but said, "Sure." He leaned on the car horn.

Half the crowd, those closest to him, turned to glance back at the source of the noise. When they saw the truck wasn't moving, they leapt into the fray again.

With a disgusted expression, Ned got out of the cab and leaned into the back of the truck to pull out his bullhorn. He pointed it at the crowd, and emitted a sirenlike noise.

Lana grinned. It sounded just like an ambulance. Startled, the entire crowd stopped to stare in his direction. Taking advantage of their momentary quiet, Ned used the bullhorn again. "Stop this nonsense. You're acting like a bunch of hoodlums instead of honest, upright citizens. Let that man go. You want to be jailed for assault?"

Everyone broke their hold on the various appendages they'd managed to grab and glanced sheepishly at Ned. He dropped the bullhorn and pointed at the people nearest him. "Is Blake Warner in there?"

The men remained sullen, but the women cried out an affirmative.

"Then let him out," Ned insisted.

Reluctantly, the mob parted and Blake appeared in the middle, looking half amused, half exasperated, and totally disheveled. Lana couldn't help but grin. It *was* kind of funny.

Blake tucked his T-shirt into his jeans and smoothed his hair, giving Ned a grin. "Thanks, buddy. All I want to do is talk to Lana."

The mayor stepped forward, his ever-present cigar apparently lost in the brawl. "She's going to marry Ned."

Melva pushed her way through the crowd. "No, she's going to marry Blake."

That started the arguing again, until Ned silenced them all with a blast of his whistle through the bullhorn. After they uncovered their ears, Ned chewed them out as if they were recalcitrant football players, telling them in no uncertain terms what he thought of their behavior. Lana stifled a grin, wondering if he was going to make them run laps or do push-ups.

He concluded by saying, "This is Lana's decision, not yours, and she's decided not to marry at all."

"Wrong," Jimmy spat out. "She'll choose a husband and set a wedding date or so she won't have a job."

"Don't forget the shower," Tommie Nell cried out, and the crowd nodded in agreement. Lana rolled her eyes. This town's obsession with showers was becoming a bit much.

"Okay," the mayor said. "She has to choose a

husband and set a date for both the shower *and* the wedding.'' Without a cigar, he had no recourse but to point his finger at Lana. ''You'll decide soon, missy, so this mess doesn't happen again.''

Who did these people think they were, dictating her life like this? Unfortunately, they might be right. Her recent failure to obtain another job was making her think twice about remaining single. Irritated, she snapped, ''I need to talk to Blake and Ned first, but I'm not going to do it in front of the whole town.''

Her two suitors, who had arranged themselves alongside her, nodded in agreement. Buoyed by their support, Lana thrust her chin higher.

''Go ahead,'' Jimmy said, gesturing toward Hazel's diner, ''but be quick about it.''

She wasn't about to have another discussion in a tiny closet. ''No, we're going to my house, where we can talk like civilized beings. I'll let you know my answer afterward.''

The mayor couldn't object to that, so Ned offered to drive Blake and Lana there, though her house wasn't very far. They accepted and Lana felt strange sandwiched in between these two men, both suitors for her hand. She didn't know why she felt that way. *They* didn't seem bothered by it at all. In fact, they seemed to be great friends. Lana might have felt better if there was more of a spirit of competition between them.

Ned glanced at Blake. ''Sorry about that. They're really good people, you know.''

''I know,'' Blake said with a grin. ''I guess I'll just have to remember to carry a bullhorn with me wherever I go.''

''It couldn't hurt,'' Ned agreed, smiling. He

glanced in the rearview mirror and his smile faded. "I don't believe it."

"What now?" Lana asked. All she needed was one more thing to go wrong today. With her luck, she'd learn Auntie Om was right all along, and there really was an alien invasion.

"They're following us."

Lana turned to look, and sure enough, people were following in cars and trucks, and there were even some stragglers trying to keep up on foot. They looked like a parade. Rolling her eyes, Lana said, "*I* believe it." But she hoped to put an end to the foolishness soon...just as soon as she made a decision.

When they reached her house, she let Blake and Ned in, then locked her doors and closed all her curtains. She wouldn't put it past anyone to peer in and she didn't want to encourage that kind of behavior. She didn't accept it from her students, and she sure wouldn't accept it from people who were supposed to be mature adults.

She waved Blake and Ned to the couch, then sat opposite them. She couldn't help but steal a few glances at Blake. He looked so good in jeans and a T-shirt that her resolve to have nothing to do with him weakened. He was enough to tempt a saint. And she was no saint.

Taking a deep breath, she decided to try one more time, hoping they'd back her up. "I told you both. I'm not planning on getting married."

The men exchanged glances, then Ned said, "You heard Jimmy. The word's out already that you're looking for a job, but no one will hire you. If you want to stay in Bachelor Falls, you'll have to choose one of us. Is that so distasteful?"

Lana stared down at her clasped hands. "No, I just want to do what's best for my baby."

Blake said, "You think it's best for the baby to have no father, to have a mother who spends all her time trying to earn a few pennies so they can eat? If you want to make a living, you'll have to leave the baby with a sitter, away from his mother for most of the day. You think *that's* best?"

His words just increased the sense of hopelessness building inside her. This is what she'd been trying to avoid thinking about. She could make it work. She knew she could. Despondent, she blurted out, "I just want my baby to be loved."

Blake gave her a reproachful look. "It's my baby, too. What makes you think I won't love it?"

"You know I'd love any child of yours," Ned added.

But what about love for *her?* That was one thing she couldn't ask for, yet she wanted it desperately. Blake didn't love her, and though Ned said he did, it wasn't the sort of passionate love she craved. It was more of a habit than anything. Ignoring the question, she said, "If I have to, I'll leave town."

"And go to a strange place where you don't know anyone?" Ned asked. "Lose the support of family and friends? Who will hire a pregnant woman?"

Turning to Blake, Lana said, "You have a large business. You could give me a job. I'll do anything."

With a look of distaste, Blake said, "And how would that look when the rest of the employees realize I was making the mother of my child work at some menial task?"

"They don't have to know."

"No," Blake said in an uncompromising tone.

"I'm not going to deny my child. But there is another alternative."

"Marriage?" she asked bitterly, knowing the answer. But maybe they were right. Maybe a loveless marriage was better than no marriage at all...if it kept her baby safe.

"Yes. Think of it as a job if you like. The job of being my child's mother, my wife, acting as my hostess."

A glorified housekeeper? No thanks. She shook her head.

Ned gave her a grave look. "Marrying either of us has to be better than living the kind of existence you're thinking about. What's your real problem?"

"Love," she blurted out. "I want to love and be loved. I want mutual passion and sharing and a home and...and..."

"It'll grow," Ned said. "We're both kinda nice guys. I'm sure you'll come to love either one of us in time."

"You don't understand," Lana said with a miserable glance at Blake. She only wanted her white knight.

Ned's eyes widened and his gaze darted toward Blake. Realization, speculation and a touch of sadness filled his expression. Suddenly she realized Ned *did* understand. Thank heavens he didn't blurt out his knowledge.

Instead he said, "The best thing for your baby is to marry one of us, don't you see that? That way you'd work only if you want to, and could spend as much time as you need with your child."

Blake nodded in agreement.

She sighed. Ned was right, though she hadn't

wanted to admit it. Marrying was the best thing for her baby, and she had to stop being selfish and thinking only of herself. Her baby would be loved no matter who she married, and would want for nothing. That wouldn't be true if she remained stubborn and single.

Suddenly she felt a weight lift from her shoulders and knew it was the right thing to do. But...who should she marry? Ned was nice, safe and he loved her, but only as a good friend. They would have peace and harmony in their home, but no passion.

She glanced at Blake, and felt the blood sing through her veins at his steady gaze. There would definitely be passion, but love? She didn't see any evidence of it.

Railing at fate, she demanded to know why she couldn't have the best of both men. But complaining wouldn't make the problem go away. She had to make a decision.

Ned interrupted her thoughts. "We'll both abide by whatever you decide."

Blake nodded. "Though whoever you choose, I'll provide support for my child. He won't want for anything if I can help it. And if you decide to marry Ned, I'd like visitation rights."

"I'll never deny you access to your child," Lana assured him.

Blake nodded in relief. "So who's—"

He broke off when they heard the door open. The mayor stuck his head in.

"How did you get in?" Lana asked.

Serena's face appeared behind Jimmy's. "I'm sorry, honey. He made me do it."

Before Lana could scold them, the mayor demanded, "So have you come to your senses?"

Lana held her chin up. "I've decided to marry, if that's what you mean."

"Good. Who?"

It seemed the whole crowd behind him held their breath, waiting for her answer. That was the question—who should she choose? She glanced at her suitors' expectant faces and knew she was no nearer to making a choice than she was before. "I don't know," she admitted.

A wave of irritation passed through the room. Lana knew they were annoyed with her, but said, "This is an important decision. I need a little more time."

Jimmy scowled. "All right, but we've set your wedding date in two weeks, the day before Bachelor Daze. Your bridal shower is next Sunday, and you have until then to decide."

Lana sighed in relief, glad for the extra time. "All right," she promised. "I'll tell you then." Maybe by then, she would have found Purple Bunny, or Blake and Ned would have magically welded together and she wouldn't have to choose.

Yeah. Fat chance.

MAYOR JIMMY BARTLETT glanced around the town hall. The group was smaller this time because he'd weeded out the troublemakers and invited only those he could trust—those right-thinking men who had as big a stake as he did in ensuring the legend of Bachelor Falls remained intact.

He called the meeting to order, saying, "As you all know, Warner got back to town today, boys." Ignoring his own role in Warner's return, Jimmy continued. "That means our plan to keep him out of Bachelor Falls is in serious jeopardy."

"Ah, why do we hafta?" Josh asked. "He seems real nice to me. He helped lots of folks last time he was here."

Jimmy glared at him with a stern expression. "I don't care how nice he is—he's gotta go or the legend will die. After Lana's hitched to Ned, Warner can come back all he wants." In fact, Jimmy would encourage it…he had some ideas for an addition to his house and wanted his opinion on it.

"He'd be gone by now if it weren't for Ned Laney," someone protested.

"Yeah," another said. "He's sabotaging our plan more than the women!"

And that's why Jimmy hadn't invited Ned to join them for this part of the meeting. "Right—Ned's too dang noble for his own good."

A chorus of "Yeah's" and nodding heads greeted his declaration. Emboldened by their agreement, Jimmy said, "We can handle a bunch of women and that city slicker, but Ned has got to go."

"Got to go? Won't that defeat the purpose?" Ralph asked.

"No, I have a plan. First, we get Ned out of town, then we distract Warner. It should be easy enough—Lana is only part of the reason he's here. The other is because of those two men. I have it on good authority that Warner didn't even know they were from his own company until yesterday. It's obvious they're up to no good, so we'll just encourage Warner to spend all his time checking them out. We'll even help, if you know what I mean."

Jimmy cast a significant glance around at the audience and saw they did indeed know what he meant. If everything went well, Warner would spend all his time trying to track these guys down.

Josh frowned. "But if he gets rid of them, won't that make him look good?"

"Not necessarily. Who's to say he didn't send them here himself to begin with, just to stir up trouble? I say let him dig his own grave and let the chips fall where they may."

"Yeah, the chips," Ralph agreed. "Besides, Ned would stop us if he knew what we were up to. But if we get him out of the way, he won't have a chance to mess us up."

It was a surprisingly logical thought for Ralph. Heads nodded at his statement, so Jimmy followed up on his advantage. "I have an idea how to do that, so I invited Ned to join us in a few moments. Back me up, will you, boys?"

"Sure," Ralph said and the rest followed suit.

A few minutes later, Ned came in and Jimmy asked him to have a seat. With a surreptitious wink at his confederates, he said, "Now that we're all here, let's get the meeting started."

Ned cocked an eyebrow. "Plotting more ways to get rid of Blake?"

"Of course not," Jimmy assured him. "We're just putting together a task force to find Lana."

"Find Lana?" Ned repeated, sounding like Ralph. "I didn't know she was missing."

"She sure is." Searching for a way to add credence to their claims, Jimmy said, "Why, Josh saw her getting on the afternoon bus. Isn't that right, Josh?" Now if only the kid would pick up on his cue.

Josh gulped, then said, "Yeah. She was crying and everything, and she wouldn't even talk to me."

Good—the kid came through. How could Ned doubt a fresh-faced boy like Josh?

"Why are you so concerned about Lana all of a sudden?"

Jimmy had an answer for that, one Ned would buy. "Because we need her back to tie the knot with you before Bachelor Daze," he blustered. "We don't want her ruinin' all our plans!"

Ned nodded slowly. "But why would she take the bus when she has a car?"

"Who knows?" Jimmy said, trying to divert attention from the weakest part of his plan. "But we have to send someone after her. We can't leave her out there, pregnant and all alone."

The other men nodded their agreement and Ned's expression turned even more concerned. "Where'd she go?"

Hank scratched his beard. "I think that bus goes clear to Little Rock, with stops in all them little towns along the way."

"Little Rock?" Ralph repeated. "Why would she be going there?"

Jimmy glared at him, willing him to shut up before he ruined everything. "Who knows? All I know is we gotta stop her and bring her back. But who'll go after her?"

"I will," Ralph said, waving his hand like a madman.

Damn. He should have explained his plan in a little more detail to Ralph. "Naw, she wouldn't listen to you. We gotta send someone she will listen to." He stuck the cigar in his mouth and assumed a puzzled expression. "Now who..."

"I'll go," Ned said. "I'm the only one she'll listen to now."

The sucker took the bait. The mayor pretended to consider his offer, then said, "You're probably right. Can we count on you to get her back here in time?"

"Of course. I want her back, too. No knowing what bee she's got in her bonnet now."

Jimmy checked his watch. "Well, you better hurry. The next bus leaves in twenty minutes."

Ned shook his head. "No need. I'll just take my truck."

"No, you have to take the bus."

"Why?"

Because that would get him out of the way longer. But Jimmy couldn't say that. Taken aback and upset he hadn't considered Ned wanting to drive himself, the mayor didn't know what to say.

Hank came to his rescue. "Do you know all them pesky little stops the bus makes?" he asked Ned.

"No, but—"

"But the bus driver does," Hank said. "And since we don't know where Lana's getting off or how far she's going, you'll have to ask at every stop if anyone's seen her."

"That's right," Jimmy said. "Surely people will remember a pretty blond pregnant lady." Before Ned could say anything more, he said, "Come on, Laney, I'm worried about Lana. You gotta make sure she's safe, but don't tell the womenfolk or we're bound to have a bunch of weepers on our hands."

The other men echoed his sentiments, and Jimmy reached for his wallet, then grabbed Ned's arm. "In fact, I've already got a round-trip ticket to Little Rock.''

Before Ned could object, Jimmy hustled him out of the town hall and down the street to the bus stop. Luckily, no one else was around. Just in time—the bus was pulling up. He didn't want to give Ned any time to think about this.

Jimmy and the others helped Ned on board with slaps on his back and urgings to find Lana and bring her home safe. Lowering his voice to avoid the attention of the interested female bus driver, Jimmy said, ''Just be back in time for the wedding.''

''What if I can't find her?'' Ned asked.

''You call me and keep in touch. If we hear from her, we'll let you know.'' He would make sure Lana was ''found'' just in time for Ned to make it back.

Ned still looked a little doubtful, so Jimmy pressed the ticket and some bills into his hand. ''Here, you'll need this for food and lodging.'' He could spare the money—it was all in a good cause.

''Okay.'' Ned hesitated, but still stepped on the bus to sit behind the driver.

As the bus pulled away, Mabel popped her head out of the diner, eyeing the group suspiciously. ''What's going on?'' she called.

''Nothing,'' Jimmy said.

''Was that Ned Laney getting on that bus?''

''Yep,'' Ralph said.

Out of the corner of his mouth, Jimmy growled, ''Ralph, keep your mouth shut. Don't say another word.''

Puzzled, Ralph repeated, ''Not a word,'' and nodded vehemently.

''What's he riding the bus for?'' Mabel wanted to

know. She was suspicious, but probably couldn't figure out why the menfolk were getting rid of their candidate for Lana's hand.

Searching for a reason she would believe, Jimmy said, "Because, uh..." Then it dawned on him. "Because he's gone to visit a girl in another town—someone who might marry him and fulfill the legend."

He could see Mabel was buying it, but she still had another question. "Why didn't he just take his truck?"

Good question. Jimmy said the first thing that popped into his mind. "It's not working."

"It was working just fine earlier."

And then he had a brainstorm. "Yeah, but since then, someone slashed his tires and put sugar in his gas tank. You wouldn't know *who,* would you?" he asked. "Like some *woman* who might not want to see him married to Lana?"

"Don't be silly," Mabel said, but she looked thoughtful and shut the door with a snap.

Josh looked at him in awe. "Wow, that was brilliant," he said in reverent tones.

Jimmy grinned and stuck the stogie in his mouth. "Yeah, it was, wasn't it? It'd take a heap of smarts to keep up with your mayor, boy, and them women just don't have it."

Feeling magnanimous now that his plan was running so smoothly, Jimmy offered to treat them all to a beer. "But first," he said, slinging his arm around Ralph's neck, "you and me need to talk, boy."

Chapter Twelve

Blake managed to slip into the Sky Hook phone booth unnoticed, feeling like a teenager sneaking into his girlfriend's bedroom. He was the CEO of a major construction company, for crying out loud. He shouldn't be reduced to this.

He called Lana, and was surprised at the wave of relief he experienced when she answered the phone. The town had kept her so busy planning the wedding and the shower that Blake hadn't been able to talk to her much, but he tried not to miss their daily conversations, even if it was only on the phone.

They'd kept him busy, too. So much so that a phone call was about all he'd been able to eke out from his busy day. Even then, he had to do it on the sly. And he still hadn't found those supposed Warner employees. Damn—Lana's spring break was being wasted.

"Hi, gorgeous," Blake said. "How's my damsel? Been in any distress lately?"

"Blake," Lana said, and the simple sound of his name echoed through him, making him feel like the knight she called him. "Good timing. Mom and her friends just left after pestering me for hours about the wedding.''

''I'm sorry to hear that. Shall I ride over on my trusty steed and smite the varlets?'' he teased.

She chuckled. ''There's no need for that. They just want to make my wedding a day to remember.''

Blake understood that. ''Yes, you deserve that at least. Have you decided who the groom will be yet?''

She paused, then said, ''No, I'm sorry, I haven't. And it's weird, but I haven't seen or heard from Ned in a couple of days.''

Despite himself, Blake felt satisfaction that his rival was missing. ''Maybe he's given up?''

''Maybe,'' Lana said, but she didn't sound convinced.

Why was he so anxious to get leg-shackled and take on another responsibility? And he *was* anxious. The thought of marrying Lana no longer held dread. In fact, he was looking forward to it. He still had to convince her, though.

Dropping the issue of Ned's whereabouts, Blake decided to press his advantage. ''I managed to keep this evening free. Would you like to do something together?''

''I'd like that,'' Lana said softly. ''But how did you manage it?''

''Oh, I just told them I was going to check out the strangers at the falls. Every time I've been there, I missed them.''

''Good idea. What did you have in mind for tonight?''

''I want it to be just you and me, alone together, with no interruptions. So, how would you like to grab some food at the Save-Rite and have dinner at your cabin?'' Dinner sounded good, but what he really wanted was to get her alone and convince her there's no way she'd ever be happy with Ned.

"I'd like that."

"Good. I'll pick you up in half an hour."

He hung up and exited the phone booth, then tracked Hank down. Wanting to give them no excuse to stop him, Blake said, "I'm heading out to Old Man Feeney's place to see if I can spot those strangers you guys keep talking about."

"You are?" Hank asked. "But, uh, I hear tell they left there half an hour ago and headed back to Branson."

The small-town grapevine was good, but not that good. Come to think of it, every time he'd missed those guys the past two days, it was after one of the locals had given him a tip. He should have realized—all he needed to do was the opposite of what they told him.

Not letting Hank know he'd caught on, Blake said, "Okay. I guess I'll just go to Mabel's Diner then." If Hank was so anxious to keep him away from that land, Blake knew he'd better check it out.

Lana didn't have any objections to stopping by the falls before dinner, so they headed out to Old Man Feeney's place. The land itself covered about twenty acres, but there was only one decent road to it. If anyone was there, they wouldn't be able to leave without Blake spotting them.

The road ended at an old house that had a small shed out back and a truck parked in front. Finally, he was in luck. "Looks like they're here this time."

Lana nodded. "Do you know who they work for?"

"No, but that's what I want to find out." Since Old

Man Feeney had moved to town to live with his daughter, Blake didn't bother with knocking on the door. Instead, he searched the area around the house while Lana investigated the pickup.

"Blake," Lana called. "Come here. I found something." She bent over the truck bed and picked up a stake. "Do you know this logo?"

He knew it all right. "Warner Construction."

"Why are they here without your knowledge?"

"I don't know, but that's another thing I intend to find out." He glanced at her dress and heels. Lana was obviously not up to traipsing around twenty acres, so he reached into the cab and leaned on the horn in a distinctive pattern that meant "come in" to all Warner employees. "That should bring them."

He and Lana settled in the car to wait and he gave her an apologetic glance. "I'm sorry this is taking so long, but I didn't authorize this. Something's fishy here and I want to get to the bottom of it."

"It's okay," she assured him. "It's kind of nice being up here all by ourselves anyway." She inhaled deeply. "Smell that? Clean, fresh air. And it's so quiet. Wouldn't it be wonderful to live up here?"

"Yes, it would," he murmured. Out here with just Lana, their baby and good fishing. He sighed. But unfortunately, his business was in Dallas and he had to live there.

They talked of inconsequential things until the men arrived. Yes, they were Warner employees all right. Their admiring gazes homed in on Lana when she and Blake got out of the car. Feeling uncharacteristically possessive, Blake wanted to shield her with his body, but managed to stop himself. He had no right...yet.

Without bothering to introduce them to Lana, he said, "Hello, Bill. Joe."

They must have recognized him finally, for they stopped and exchanged a sheepish glance. "Damn," Bill said. "We've been trying to avoid you."

Taken aback by his candor, Blake said, "You knew I was here?"

"Yes, your father told us, but he wanted this to be a surprise."

Did he now? "Well, someone let the cat out of the bag, so I thought I'd come up and see how you're getting along," Blake said, fishing for information.

"Great," Joe said. "Your father said you always wanted a resort here. You're right—it's a fabulous spot for it. Come see."

He led them over to the truck and took out some preliminary sketches and spread them across the hood. "The main hotel will be here, with a golf course, tennis courts, a restaurant, swimming pool, nature trails, the works. We'll have to remove some trees, but that shouldn't be too difficult."

Some trees? Hell, they were planning to denude half the site. Lana stared at him, appalled, and Blake shook his head in warning. If they denounced the plans too soon, he'd never learn anything.

He pointed to a spot on the sketch. "What's this?"

"It's a man-made lake," Joe said with unfeigned enthusiasm. "If we divert the river a bit, we'll be able to have a huge area for water sports and the like."

"I see," Blake murmured. "Do you plan to beef up the road system in Bachelor Falls to handle the heavy traffic?"

"There's no need," Bill assured him. "See here?

We'll build a new road to bypass the town entirely and go right to Branson.''

"What about the impact on Bachelor Falls?"

They seemed surprised. "Well, we'll create a lot of new jobs so it's gotta be good—progress, you know."

They looked at him expectantly and Blake forced himself to smile. His definition of progress didn't mesh with theirs. It might create a few jobs, but the resort would be self-contained, so it wouldn't provide much additional income for the town after it was built. In fact, that bypass would draw people away from Bachelor Falls. And what they planned to do to the local environment resembled destruction more than progress.

He wouldn't take it out on these guys. They were just doing what they were told, but he had to nip this in the bud. "Thanks for the report, guys. So when are you going to close on the land?"

"Oh, that's already done," Bill said. "Your father pushed it through fast so we wouldn't waste any time."

Blake's jaw tightened in frustration. This had gone further than he'd expected. "I see. Well, thank you again. We'll leave you alone now so you can get on with your work."

"Great," Joe said. "And I'm glad you know about it now so we can come up here anytime we want."

When they got back into the car and pulled out, Lana demanded, "Did you know about this?"

"No. If I had, I would've stopped it."

"Then why didn't you tell them to stop now?"

"I need to make some phone calls and get more information before I can do anything." He gave her an apologetic look. "Looks like we won't be able to do the cabin this evening after all." It didn't have a phone.

Lana nodded. "That's okay. Do what you have to—just stop them. You can use my phone and I'll whip us up something for dinner."

He breathed a sigh of relief. She understood. "Thanks, I'd appreciate that."

When they reached her house, he parked in the garage so no one would see his car. He called Grace, but she didn't know anything about the land deal, so while Blake munched on a quick meal, he called everyone he could think of who was still loyal to him. Slowly, a picture emerged.

Throughout it all, Lana just watched. When he hung up from talking to the accounting department, he sighed.

"Have you figured out what's going on yet?" she asked.

"I've just been able to confirm what we already know. Everything was done hush-hush, on the premise that it was something I wanted but didn't have the time to pursue. My father touted it as a surprise gift to me for the ten years of service I've put into the company. That's how he was able to keep me in the dark."

"But you're the CEO. Wouldn't you have found out about it sooner or later?"

"Yes, but a lot later, when it was too late to stop it."

"It's not too late now?"

"No, I can still stop it, but I'd like to know *why* Dad is doing this." For the life of him, he couldn't figure it out.

"Why don't you call and ask him?"

He stared at her in surprise. "I guess I could. Good idea—I'll do that."

He called and found his father at home. Without preamble, Blake asked, "What's going on with this Bachelor Falls resort project?"

"What project?" his father asked in a wary voice.

"The one you're keeping secret from me."

"I don't know what you're talking about," he blustered. "Where did you hear such a thing?"

"That's not important. What's important is that I did hear about it and I'd like an explanation."

"Well, you're not going to get one from me. I know nothing about it."

So his father had resorted to lying. "Bull. What are you trying to pull, Dad? I know damned good and well that you instigated this project without my knowledge, and I'd like to know why."

"Are you calling me a liar?"

If the shoe fits... "Well, you're not telling the truth."

Livid now, his father yelled into the phone. "How dare you? I'll have you know that you may be CEO but *I* still own this company, and I can do any damn thing I want. And I sure as hell don't need your permission."

Before Blake could respond, his father slammed the phone down. Blake winced. "Well, that was real productive."

"He didn't admit to it?" Lana asked.

"No. Damn it, if only I was there, I could figure out what's really going on."

The instant disappointment on her face made him feel like a heel. He'd come out here to convince her to marry him, and now he proposed to run back to Dallas at the first sign of a problem. Seen from her point of view, he didn't seem like a really good candidate for marriage.

Maybe he could rearrange his priorities. "Then again, I'm sure Grace can handle this."

The hope in Lana's expression convinced him it was the right thing to do. He'd rather take care of this himself, but he knew he could count on Grace to do whatever needed to be done. He called her again.

"Grace? Hi, it's Blake. Listen, I found out this Bachelor Falls deal is definitely on, but my father disavows all knowledge of it."

"You mean he lied," Grace said flatly.

It didn't seem to surprise her as much as it had him. "Right, but I don't know why. Regardless, I think we can stop this."

"How?"

"I need you to contact all those involved, and see what you can do to kill this project—quick."

"Me?" she asked in surprise. "Aren't you coming back?"

"No, I need to stay here and iron some things out."

Lana smiled at him and he grinned back at her, hoping he was doing the right thing.

"Okay, you're the boss," Grace said. "Are you sure you know what you're doing?"

"Yes, that's why I made you vice president. That'll give you the leverage to throw your weight around a little."

"I'd feel a whole lot better if you were here."

"You'll do fine. And if you have any questions, you can call me here anytime, okay?"

"Okay," Grace responded and they hung up.

Lana beamed at him and came over to give him a hug and a kiss on the cheek.

"What's that for?" he asked.

"For saving the town...and for being such a white knight."

It felt good to be on the receiving end of her approval. "But I ruined our evening."

She smiled and settled her soft curves into his lap. "Yes, but there's still some of it left. What do you say we make the most of it?"

"Good idea—" He broke off when he heard the doorbell ring. "Ignore that," he advised.

Too late. Serena stuck her head in the door and, disregarding the sight of her daughter in his lap, said, "Oh, good, there you are, Blake."

He sighed, wondering what she wanted now.

"Ona Mae heard some more scratching and is worried about the locks you installed."

"They're perfectly good dead bolts," he said. "They should keep out any Bostians and other alien creatures."

Serena gave him a sympathetic glance. "I know that, and you know that, but the problem is convincing Ona Mae. She had a dream that the strangers out at the falls are Bostians coming to get her and the only way to calm her is to have you check her locks."

He glanced at Lana. She smiled ruefully. "Maybe you'd better go to her. She'll fret all night if you don't."

"It will probably take all evening," he warned.

"I know. Maybe we can try again tomorrow night?"

"Yes, we'll do that." She slid off his lap and he

stood, grimacing at Serena. "Take me to your leader."

AFTER A LONG DAY of making endless decisions about the wedding, Lana went by the school to pick up a few things. When she left, she was looking forward to a nice evening alone with Blake. That is, if they could manage to escape before someone cornered them.

She heard a car pull into the parking lot behind her, but refused to look in that direction, acting as if she didn't hear whoever it was. She bent to unlock her door and heard a voice behind her.

"Psst. Hey, lady, you want a ride?"

She knew that voice. Turning, she smiled at Blake. He leaned across the front seat of his car to grin up at her through the window.

Pretending to consider, she tapped a finger on her chin. "I don't know. Can you be trusted?"

He laid a hand over his heart. "Absolutely." He pointed to the back seat where a picnic basket sat. "And if you're a good little girl, I'll even give you some candy."

"I don't really care for candy," she demurred.

He leered. "Well, how about Hazel's pot roast, then?"

"Hmm...much better." She got in the car and dropped the game. "How'd you know I was here?"

"Your mother told me. I've been hiding until I saw you come out."

She chuckled at the mental picture of Blake peeking out from behind the trees. "Does this mean we're actually going to get away this time?"

"I hope so. Tonight I promise no interruptions."

"How?"

"Well, Hazel's helping by convincing Ralph I'm snaking her drains tonight."

"Good old Hazel," Lana said, chuckling.

"Yes. Even better, we don't have to stop anywhere along the way and risk someone catching us. It was her idea to send food."

"Great." Lana relaxed and enjoyed the rest of the drive, unwinding from her stressful day.

When they got to the cabin, Blake wouldn't let her help. Instead, he insisted she lie down on the couch and rest for a few moments. Indulging him because she was tired, Lana closed her eyes and let the stress drain away. Some time later, she felt a feather-soft touch on her cheek and woke to find Blake smiling down at her.

He kissed her softly, then withdrew and held out his hand. "Dinner's ready."

She let him lead her to the table and gasped in delight. He'd covered the rustic picnic table with a snowy white tablecloth and set it with fine china, silver and crystal. Soft music played in the background and slim tapers lit the scene, flanking a single red rose in an elegant vase.

A candlelight dinner? No one had ever done anything so special for her. "Oh, Blake," she said on a sigh. "It's beautiful."

He shrugged off her praise, but his smile widened. "I'm glad you like it."

He held her chair until she sat, then draped a towel over his arm and produced a bottle with a flourish, presenting it to her. "If Madame approves?"

She glanced at the label. Nonalcoholic wine. Delighted that he was so thoughtful and concerned for their baby, she said, "Madame definitely approves."

He poured two glasses, then sat and extended his glass. "A toast."

She raised hers, wondering what form his toast would take.

"To...our baby. May he be healthy, intelligent and one hell of a football player."

She chuckled. "To our baby," she agreed, and took a sip. She'd been afraid he would try to toast to their marriage, thus forcing her to choose between him and Ned right now, but he'd surprised her once more by being kind and considerate. "But it might be a girl."

"Then may she be healthy, intelligent and one hell of a woman...just like her mother."

Lana melted and her mouth trembled upward in a smile as their gazes locked. What was that expression in his eyes? Caring, sincerity, tenderness and... something else. She couldn't name it and doubted he could either. Could it be love?

He broke off first, saying, "Well, better eat before our dinner gets cold." He slid two plates out of the oven and placed them on the table.

They ate and exchanged small talk until they could eat no more. Lana rose, saying, "We'd better clean up, I guess."

"Not now," he said, and took her hand. "We'll do that later. Come, I want to talk to you."

He led her to the couch and cuddled her close. She sighed, feeling safe and comforted, yet a little apprehensive. "What did you want to talk about?" she asked in a wary tone.

"You." He spread his hand over her belly. "The baby. What's going on in that body of yours?"

Surprised, she asked, "You really want to know?"

Still keeping his hand over her abdomen, he said, "Yes, of course. That's my baby growing inside there. I want to know what's going on with him...or her. I want to understand what's going on with *you*."

Charmed by his interest, she said, "What do you want to know first?"

She felt a movement in her abdomen and Blake's eyes grew round. "Was that the baby?" he whispered.

"Yes," she whispered back. "I think so."

Blake grinned. "Wow. Quite a little kicker for such a little guy, isn't he?"

Lana chuckled. It hadn't seemed like such a large movement to her, but if Blake wanted to act the proud father, far be it from her to complain. "I don't know," she admitted. "This is the first time I've felt him move."

"Really? I'm glad I could share this first time with you."

"Me, too." She allowed herself to dream for a moment, envisioning them sharing many more first moments together...the baby's first smile, first tooth, walking, going to school. Her imagination even stretched as far as the first date and wedding, even...grandchildren.

Blake's voice brought her back to the here and now. "So what else is going on inside you right now?"

"Well, I thought for some reason that only my belly would be affected, but pregnancy is a whole body experience."

"How so?"

He seemed truly interested so she went on to explain as much as she knew about enlarged breasts, weight gain everywhere, stretch marks, loosened joints and that strange dark line down the center of her abdomen. She even found herself describing those things she had only confided to her doctor, such as increased gas, constipation, dizziness, early nausea and now constant hunger.

"Good Lord," he exclaimed. "All that?"

She'd become so involved in telling Blake everything that she hadn't noticed his increasing horror. When she did, she decided not to downplay it. "Yes, and it will only get worse as it goes on."

He shuddered. "How do you stand it?"

She smiled. "I stand it because I know I'm carrying a precious human being inside me...our baby."

He nodded, and she thought he understood. "Aren't you scared?" he asked.

"Terrified. Not of labor, but I'm afraid I'm going to do something wrong, something that will hurt our baby." Especially since Purple Bunny was still missing.

"The Pregnancy Police don't help. I don't know why they feel obligated to tell me horror stories about other births. And they tell me I can't raise my arms above my head or I'll strangle the baby with the cord, or scramble his brains with the microwave, or give him cancer by eating peanut butter."

"You're kidding. Is that true?"

She laughed. "No. But just in case, I've been reading up on pregnancy and talking to Dr. Evans."

"You can't be too careful. Do you think everything will be okay? With you *and* the baby, I mean."

She patted his hand in reassurance. "Yes, I'm doing fine. It's not a high-risk pregnancy, and the doctor says I'm very healthy and should have no problems."

"They sound like problems to me," he exclaimed.

"Well, except for the normal signs of pregnancy, I mean. Don't worry. I'm having all the right tests done, even going to Springfield when Dr. Evans doesn't have the proper equipment."

"Good." He seemed relieved.

Suddenly her tiredness overtook her and she yawned.

"Being tired is one of the side effects, too, isn't it?"

"I'm afraid so. Not to mention the fact that I had a very busy day."

He cuddled her closer, though he didn't remove his hand from her tummy. "Me, too. These odd jobs are beginning to wear me out."

Appalled, she said, "I'm sorry, I didn't think. The town is taking advantage of you, just like your family, by putting additional responsibilities on your shoulders."

"Not really. I don't mind."

"You don't? Why?"

"I don't know," he said with a shrug. "It's different somehow. Maybe it's because the people here seem to really need my help, even when I know they're just trying to keep me away from you. And maybe it's because they're so...grateful for the smallest things."

Ah, that explained it. His family *expected* it of him and the people here didn't. And she doubted his family had expressed anything so polite as gratitude.

There was another difference, too. Bachelor Falls,

with all its faults, was winning him over. Despite himself, she sensed he was coming to love it.

She hugged that thought to herself and snuggled closer. With sudden insight, she realized that this evening had also shown her much more—he was also coming to love her, too.

Even if he didn't know it yet.

THE MEN OF BACHELOR FALLS met in secret once more, sneaking out early in the morning when few people would be suspicious. Jimmy glowered at his fellow conspirators. "Where's Ned?" he growled.

Ralph shrugged. "Ned? Still on the bus, I reckon."

"Hasn't anyone heard from him?"

No one fessed up. "Then we have a problem, men."

"Yeah, a problem," Ralph echoed. "Uh, what is it?"

Jimmy glared at him. "Blake and Lana disappeared last night and didn't come home until late—together. And that's after he spent the evening with her the night before. We can't have that. Wasn't it your turn to watch him?"

"I *did* watch him, right up to the moment he went to help Hazel snake her drains," Ralph said defensively.

"You dolt. It wasn't Hazel's drains he was snakin'—it was Lana's."

"I-I didn't know."

"He's too slippery. He snuck out the back while you were enjoying pie and ice cream."

"Hazel makes the best blueberry pie," Ralph muttered, as if that made it all right.

The mayor stabbed his cigar in Ralph's direction.

"Well, we can't have any more of this...drain-snakin' business."

"That's your fault," Hank piped up. "If you hadn't put Ned on that bus, he'd be here givin' Blake some competition."

"No, he'd be here messin' up his own chances," Jimmy snapped back. Couldn't they see the obvious?

Hank snorted. "If that's so, why do you want him back now?"

"Dang it, I thought he'd be back by now, or at least called so we could persuade him to come home. How's it gonna look tomorrow at the shower when Lana has to choose a husband and her best choice isn't even there?"

The men nodded, finally understanding. "What are we going to do about it?" Josh asked, showing proper concern.

"Well, we won't let Ralph watch him again, that's for sure. It's your turn tomorrow, Josh. Make sure he don't get too close to Lana, you hear?"

Josh nodded and Jimmy turned to a pouting Ralph. "You can help, too. Find Ned for me."

"Find Ned?" Ralph repeated with a squeak. "How?"

Shoot, couldn't he think for himself? "I don't know—call the bus company, all the stations along the route. Do anything you have to, but find him and get him back here as soon as possible."

Hank frowned. "But what if he can't make it back tomorrow and Lana chooses Blake?"

Jimmy thrust the cigar back in his mouth and bit down hard. "We'll just have to deal with that if it happens."

Chapter Thirteen

Blake eased into the town hall late the next afternoon, trying to hide behind one of the large white honeycomb bells. No such luck. Unlike the last shower, he knew almost everyone here by name, and they knew him. They also knew he would learn today if Lana was going to choose him or not.

He hated the thought of waiting for Lana's decision in front of a crowd, especially *this* crowd. They all cast speculative, encouraging or annoyed glances at him, depending on which side of the legend controversy they championed.

Serena hurried to his side. "Don't worry, Blake. I'm sure Lana will choose you."

Her hands fluttered around him like demented moths at a flame. Obviously, she *wasn't* sure. It didn't reassure him. In fact, it just made him as nervous as...well, as a suitor waiting for the answer to his marriage proposal.

He'd done everything he could to convince Lana to marry him, short of carrying her off by force. He no longer balked at the idea of marriage to her. She was beautiful, loving, kind, passionate—and the only person he knew who didn't pressure him, didn't ask anything of him. Oddly enough, she was the only one he really *wanted* to help, yet she didn't really seem to need him.

That wasn't quite true. Grace said Lana needed love, but he couldn't promise her that. But if he could love anyone, it would be Lana. She filled in those parts of him he hadn't known were missing with her peaceful disposition and simple acceptance. His only concern was that, with her generous nature, she might get sucked into the same trap with him—virtual servitude to the whims of his family. He wanted to protect her from them, keep her safe and insulated from their demands. But...would he be able to?

Of course, he might be worrying in vain. She still could choose Ned over him. So where the heck was she?

There was a commotion at the front door and Lana walked in, looking more beautiful and radiant than he'd ever seen her before. Pregnancy definitely agreed with her, despite the horror stories she'd told him yesterday.

As everyone greeted her with a shower of rose petals, Blake realized with a start that she was wearing the same lavender-flowered dress she'd worn the day they met, the one he'd had so much pleasure in removing from her that fateful night. Was this a sign?

Blake felt rooted to the spot, unable to move as Lana stood calmly in the doorway.

The mayor stepped over to her, shoved his cigar in his mouth and growled, "No more shilly-shallying now. The time has come to choose a husband. Who's it gonna be?"

Lana opened her mouth, but was forestalled by a voice from the back. "Wait, Ned's not here."

Damn it, who cared? Why didn't they just let her speak and get it over with?

Looking surprised, Lana glanced over the crowd. She spotted Blake and gave him a half smile. What did that mean? Was she glad to see him...or only trying to soften the coming blow?

"Yes," Lana said, "where is Ned?"

Looking annoyed, Jimmy said, "He had a family emergency...out of town. But he wanted to be here—he asked me to tell you that he plans on being here for the wedding."

Yeah, yeah, get on with it, Blake urged silently.

"I'm sorry to hear that," Lana said.

"So who's it to be?"

Lana paused and the crowd went still as everyone seemed to hold their breath, no one more so than Blake.

She smiled and thrust her chin in the air. "I choose Blake."

Blake's heart did a somersault, but he remained paralyzed until Serena gave him an encouraging shove. He strode to Lana's side, skirting the scowling mayor to sweep her into his arms and claim her lips in a soul-satisfying kiss. The women cheered and the men grumbled, but Blake didn't care. Lana had chosen him!

He let her go, grinning at the sight of her blush, and reached into his pocket to bring out a small jeweler's box. He pulled out the diamond solitaire and slipped it on the third finger of her left hand amidst another shower of rose petals from the enthusiastic women. "Thank you for choosing me. I—I..."

She gazed up at him with expectation. "Yes, Blake? You what?"

"I...hope you won't regret this."

Whispering, "So do I," she lowered her head to gaze down at the ring, twisting it so the facets caught the light. Her lower lip quivered as her eyes turned moist.

"What's wrong?" he asked.

She swiped a tear away and said, "Nothing. I—I didn't expect this. It's beautiful. When did you get it?"

"Right before you came to Dallas."

"You were so sure of me?"

He couldn't tell if she were angry or teasing. "No, I just hoped."

She smiled then and he would have resumed their embrace, but Serena pulled them apart, beaming. "That's enough. You'll have plenty of time for that later. Right now you have presents to open."

Relieved that was over, Blake played second fiddle to Lana for the rest of the shower, letting her take center stage. He made appropriate comments over the gifts, but was more interested in watching her. She seemed somewhat melancholy, almost sad. Wondering what was wrong, he decided to find out later when they were alone.

Eventually the shower ended, and Blake helped her carry the packages to their cars. As they passed the mayor at the door, Jimmy said, "I think you're making a big mistake, Lana. Ned's the man for you."

Lana shot Blake a warning stare so he kept his mouth shut. As the victor he could afford to be magnanimous.

"I think I chose correctly," Lana said softly.

Jimmy scowled at Blake. "Humph. He probably

won't even show up. If his daddy calls or the business needs him, he'll be out of here like a shot.''

Lana gave Blake an unsure look, but told Jimmy, ''He'll be there. You forced me to make a choice and I did. Now live with it.'' Without giving him a chance to reply, she swept out the door, head held high.

Blake grinned and spoke to Jimmy. ''She's right. Your boy lost, so give it up. Lana's mine now and I won't tolerate any more interference. Understood?''

Jimmy bit down so hard on his stogie he cut it in two. Spitting out the severed end, he said, ''It ain't over yet, Warner. You still gotta get hitched.''

''Oh, I will,'' Blake said, and followed Lana out the door.

When they got back to her house and unloaded the presents, she made him dinner. The meal was a quiet affair, with Lana in a strange, pensive mood. What was bugging her? Blake searched his mind for what he could have said or done to put her in this mood. Was it what Jimmy said?

Blake followed her into the kitchen and they stacked their dishes in the sink. When she would have washed them, he stopped her. ''That can wait. Let's talk.''

''All right.''

They went back into the living room and sat on the couch together. Lana seemed a little reticent so he tugged on a lock of her hair. ''Why are you suddenly so shy?''

She shrugged but didn't look at him. ''I don't know. I've only been engaged once before.''

''It's a new experience for me, too.'' He raised her chin with a finger. ''Now tell me what's really wrong. Are you afraid I won't show up?''

"Not really."

"Then you have some doubt." Before she could say anything, he said, "Lana, I won't let the business or my family come between us, I promise."

She nodded, and fixed him with wide, questioning eyes. "I know, but...have you told your family about us yet?"

"Not yet." He'd rather present them with a *fait accompli*.

"Don't you think you should? You can use my phone. Maybe they'd like to come to the wedding."

She didn't sound any more confident of that than he was, but he knew he had to call them if only to set her mind at rest. He'd much rather do it when she wasn't listening, but he had no choice in the matter. Giving her a false smile, he said, "Sure. I'll call them now."

He dialed his parents' number, hoping they wouldn't be there. Unfortunately they were. "Hello, Mother."

"Blake? Is something wrong?"

"No, nothing's wrong. In fact, I have good news." At least, he hoped she'd take it that way. He glanced at Lana and she returned his encouraging smile with a steady expression that hinted she knew exactly what was going on in his mind.

"What good news?" his mother asked.

"I'm getting married."

"To whom?"

Bravely he said, "To Lana Talbot," with as cheerful a voice as he could manage.

"To *her?*" she shrieked. "How could you?" He heard the muffled sound of her voice as she turned away from the phone to say, "Blake is marrying that hick. Here, do something."

Blake smiled reassuringly at Lana as his father's voice came on the line. "Is this true?" the elder Warner demanded.

"Yes, isn't it great?"

"Like hell it is. I had a bad feeling a month ago when I heard you were taking a vacation in the back of beyond. You can't do this to us. We have someone else all picked out for you. That girl is a nobody."

"She's my fiancée," Blake reminded him with a thread of steel in his voice.

"Not for long if I have anything to say about it."

"You don't," Blake said calmly. Though he was seething, he had to keep up appearances for Lana's sake. She didn't deserve this.

"The hell I don't," his father thundered. "I knew this was coming—that's why I bought that land."

"I thought you didn't know anything about it."

Ignoring him, his father went on to say, "If you marry her, I'll build the resort and ruin the whole damn town. Then what will she think of you?"

His father knew what the resort would do to Bachelor Falls and he *still* planned to build it? He was even more unscrupulous than Blake had thought. Well this time he wasn't going to let the old man intimidate him. "Not if I win the Palladian bid. Then the company is mine and you promised to forfeit all rights to it."

"Not all. Not this part."

"What do you mean?" Was he going to welsh on their deal?

"I promised to keep out of *your* projects, but this is my own personal project. So, it doesn't matter if you win the bid or not. You marry that woman and I'll destroy her town.''

Blake's mind whirled, trying to find some way to stop this catastrophe. ''Do you have a contract to build a resort there?''

''No, but I'll get one.''

''How? We don't have the funds for that, and it's not a good location or a good investment.''

''Then we'll operate it.''

''We're a construction company,'' Blake protested. ''We don't know anything about resort management.'' Seeing nothing ahead but disaster, he said, ''If you do this, we'll lose the company.''

''That'll be on your head,'' his father replied, unconcerned. ''You know how to stop it.''

Knowing there was nothing he could do about it here and now, Blake unclenched his jaw and said, ''I can't do that. And, as CEO, I wouldn't recommend you take this course.''

''You have no say,'' his father taunted. ''I'm still the major stockholder.''

''Until I win the bid, you mean.''

''Even if you do, this project is still all mine. Besides, you've been gone so long, you don't have a chance in hell of winning that bid.''

Damn—that sounded as if he knew something Blake didn't. What was the old man up to now? Had he stooped to sabotaging his own company just to win the bet? Blake hadn't thought it possible, but now he wasn't so sure. Speaking with confidence, he said, ''Grace handled it. She's very sharp.''

His father laughed derisively. ''Go on believing that. My victory will be even sweeter then.''

Blake wanted to let him know exactly what he

thought of him, but a lifetime of obedience coupled with Lana's presence made him cool his temper.

Hoping he could sway him with the promise of what he'd always wanted, Blake said, "I have more good news."

"You've changed your mind?"

"No, I'm going to be a father. You're going to be a grandfather."

"So that's what this is all about. You fool—you don't have to get married just because you got the girl pregnant. I'll give you whatever's necessary to get rid of it and buy her silence."

Get rid of it? How could his father be so callous about his own grandchild—the grandchild his mother had been bugging him to produce for years? Knowing Lana was listening, Blake said, "I don't think that will be necessary. Oh, and the wedding is a week from today. I hope you can make it."

His father spluttered, but Blake hung up on him. If he kept on with this conversation, he was going to blow his top and he didn't want to do that in front of Lana.

Damn. Now what was he going to do? If he married Lana, the town would be destroyed.

This was the worst possible time for a wedding.

LANA HAD ONLY HEARD half of the conversation but she knew something was wrong. Despite Blake's control, she sensed his parents weren't at all happy about the news. Well, at least it appeared they hadn't swayed him.

She glanced down at her engagement ring, unused to the unaccustomed weight on her finger. She didn't quite know what to make of Blake. Sometimes he could be incredibly sweet and romantic, like buying her this ring and fixing her the candlelight dinner. Other times she wondered about him.

When he'd stuttered this afternoon after she chose him, she'd expected something else to come out of his mouth. Okay, so she was dumb to hope for a declaration of love...but couldn't he at least have said he was happy they were getting married?

Lana raised her head when Blake hung the phone up. His face was grim.

"They hate the idea, don't they?" she asked calmly.

He scowled and she could tell he was wondering whether to tell her the truth and hurt her feelings or lie. "The truth, please."

"They're not crazy about it," he admitted. "But it's not really you they have a problem with. It's more the fact that they like to control every aspect of my life, and by making this decision without their consent, I've defied them."

It's about time. Gently she said, "They take advantage of you, treat you like a servant, not a son." And Blake let them do it.

He frowned. "They're my family."

Maybe she should keep her mouth shut, but she hated to see what they were doing to him. "I know they are...and I'll be your family, too."

He looked surprised, as if that hadn't occurred to him. "What are you trying to say?"

"In a week I'll be your wife, which makes me part of your family." She hesitated. "That is, if you're still planning to marry me." She said it with trepidation, hoping he wouldn't take it as an invitation to renege. But if he was going to jilt her, she wanted to know now, not when she was standing at the altar.

"Yes, of course I still plan to marry you."

His voice didn't quite ring true. "But...?"

"But something's come up at the office." Running a hand over his face, Blake said, "I gotta be honest with you. My father did buy Old Man Feeney's land." He clasped his hands and stared down at them. "He's planning to build the resort if I don't do what he says."

Shocked, Lana asked, "Why?"

"To spite me. He knows it will ruin Bachelor Falls and the company, but he doesn't care."

The man was unbelievable. "What does he want you to do?"

"Jilt you."

Dear Lord, Blake's father hated her so much, he was willing to destroy the town she loved and the company Blake had poured his heart and soul into? "Maybe it's best if we don't marry, then."

"No, we'll marry," Blake said with a stubborn expression. "I didn't realize until today how much I've let him control me. I can't let it continue."

"Do you need to be there?"

"I wish I could," he admitted.

"Are you going, then?" she asked with a sinking feeling, knowing how important this was to him.

He paused and she could see his internal struggle. Finally he said, "No, I'll call Grace and have her handle it. She's more than capable."

Lana was glad he wanted to stay near her, but... "I can't let our marriage ruin Bachelor Falls—or your life."

"You'd rather my father just ruined yours?"

"It doesn't have to be ruined," she said softly. "I could still marry Ned." It wouldn't be the same, but what else could she do? She still had her baby to think of.

Blake's answer was immediate and emphatic. "No. I *want* to marry you, and damn it, I'm going to."

She took a deep breath, knowing she had to let him go, even if she hated it. "I can't let you do that."

"Yes, you can. I've been thinking. Once I win this bid and get back to Dallas, I'm sure I'll find a way to kill the resort. Besides, I doubt he'll really go through with it."

"What if he does? How will you stop him?"

"I don't know yet—I need to check out the situation first. If necessary, I'll have him declared incompetent." Blake captured her hand and squeezed it with a reassuring grip. "Don't worry, I won't let this happen."

He didn't sound as confident as she would have wished, but he obviously meant it. Lana relented. "I hope so."

"Great. Well, I guess I'd better call Grace and warn her what's up."

"Okay." Lana rose to give him some privacy. "I'll just do the dishes."

After she washed the dishes, Lana waited at the kitchen table for Blake to finish his conversation and glanced down at her hand where the winking diamond mocked her.

She ought to be ecstatic. She'd just gotten engaged to the man she loved. But instead she felt nothing but dread and despair.

How could she feel otherwise when his father loathed her so much he was willing to take such drastic measures to ensure Blake didn't marry her? And though Blake said he wanted to be her husband, he didn't even hint that he might love her. Last night, she'd been so sure he was beginning to feel that way, but after today, she wasn't so sure. And now, the prospect of living in Dallas with his disapproving parents and that cold apartment was even more daunting.

She shook her head, admonishing herself to remember that this is what was best for her baby. She'd just have to make the best of it, that was all.

That is, if Blake even showed up for the wedding. What if he couldn't find a way to stop his father or win that bid between now and then? He'd chosen his company over her before by returning to Dallas. Who was to say he wouldn't do it again?

Blake came into the kitchen and Lana looked up. "Did you reach Grace?"

He joined her at the table. "Yes."

"How'd it go?"

He rubbed the back of his neck. "Well, unfortunately the bid opening is the day after the wedding."

"Oh." Here it came. "The mayor won't let me change the date." She'd only been engaged a few hours, and already it was over. Trying not to cry, Lana twisted off her ring. Where the hell was Purple Bunny when she needed him?

"I know." He glanced down at her hands. "What are you doing?"

She shrugged, trying to appear nonchalant, as if it weren't ripping her insides out. She offered him the solitaire. "Giving you back your ring."

He took it, but only to haul her to her feet and shove the ring back on with a grimace. "No—that's where it belongs, and that's where it's gonna stay."

She blinked back tears. "But, the bid—"

"I've got that covered," he said. "Grace is sending me a cell phone so I can keep in touch to answer any last-minute questions." He hugged her. "Don't worry," he whispered fiercely. "I'll be there."

She rested her head on his shoulder and let the tears come. *I hope so.*

THE MAYOR CALLED another secret meeting to order.

"What's going on?" Ralph asked. "I thought you said Ned was coming back."

Jimmy took the cigar out of his mouth. "No, you nitwit. I lied. I just said I'd heard from him so Lana wouldn't think Ned had changed his mind about marrying her."

"Oh."

As Ralph looked downcast, Hank raised his hand. "But the fact is, he ain't here, and Lana's done gone and picked Blake. What are we going to do now?"

"They're not hitched yet," the mayor reminded them. "And we still have a week until the wedding to turn things around."

"How?"

"Well, first we need to find Ned. Since Ralph hasn't had any luck, I figure we need some volunteers to drive out and find him. Check all the bus stations, all the hospitals, all the hotels and motels between here and Little Rock. Who's game?"

Several men volunteered and Jimmy divvied up the territory each was to search and sent them on their way, admonishing them to get back in time for the wedding. The only one he ignored was Ralph.

Looking put out, Ralph said, "Don't you trust me?"

Not on a complex mission like this. "I need you for the second part of the plan, along with Hank and Josh."

"Second part?" he asked eagerly.

"It's not enough to find Ned and get him back here. We gotta make sure Warner doesn't make it to the altar."

Ralph's eyes opened wide. "You want us to kill him?"

"Of course not!" He'd better spell this out very carefully or Ralph would screw it up again. "Now here's what we're gonna do...."

Chapter Fourteen

Blake spent the next week taking care of all the nit-picky details associated with getting married. He hadn't realized there was so much to it—special clothing, rehearsals, a license, a preacher, rings, not to mention the thousand other details he was consulted about like flowers, colors and whatnot.

Wistfully he wished he and Lana could just take off and go fishing. He didn't care what color ribbons went on the bouquet or how many bags of birdseed they needed, but he knew Lana did so he put up with it for her sake.

Now that she had chosen him, the men had to let him see her, but they weren't happy about it. They still found excuses to disturb them as often as possible so Lana and Blake didn't have much time alone. The women were just as bad, hovering around Lana with endless lists, swatches of material and other things he couldn't begin to comprehend. And everything seemed more complicated by the fact that Lana wanted to be married at the falls.

What little free time he had, he spent in trying to find a way to prevent his father from building the resort. The cell phone helped, permitting him to do two things at once, not to mention allowing him to escape from Hank's and Esther's inquisitiveness.

Until this mess with his father was resolved, he and Lana would have to forego their honeymoon, which meant they'd leave the day after the wedding to head back to Dallas. Lana had found someone to take over her job for the small part of the school year still remaining, but he wasn't so lucky.

The only consolation would be that this whole goat-rope would finally be over and he and Lana could be alone without the entire population of Bachelor Falls watching their every move. That is, unless he managed to blow it again somehow.

But first things first. He had to get through this shindig tonight. Why the mayor insisted on giving him a bachelor party, Blake had no clue. The only man in town who seemed to approve of this marriage was Ned—and Blake hadn't seen him in over a week.

He walked down to the town hall, pushed open the door, and acknowledged the boisterous greetings as the men sang along with loud country-western music. It appeared they'd started without him.

He glanced around the hall and suppressed a grin at the mayor's idea of a bachelor party. The refreshments consisted of one keg of beer and a few bowls of pretzels with chips and dip.

Some of the guys dragged him over to a chair and shoved a mug of beer in his hand, then proposed a toast to his marriage. Wondering why they were suddenly so affable, Blake sipped and they encouraged him to drink up.

The light dawned. They wanted to get him so drunk and hung over he wouldn't be able to make it tomorrow. To foil their plans, Blake tried to keep his alcohol-intake low, but every time his mug emptied someone refilled it. Surreptitiously he began dumping it in a nearby plant.

This went on for an hour, with bawdy jokes and unsolicited marital advice, until Jimmy called for the entertainment. Blake had to stifle a laugh when a blonde in pigtails came bouncing out in a cheerleader uniform and began to dance. Well, it was more of a cheer routine than a dance, but the guys seemed to love it.

They hooted and hollered as the ditzy Belinda pranced, kicked and jiggled all around the room, never taking off a stitch of clothes. He smiled to be polite, but wished she'd stop. Her gyrations were making him nauseous.

Finally, when he thought he could endure no more, Belinda bobbed a couple of small curtseys and cartwheeled out of the room. Over the cheering of the crowd, Blake heard his cell phone buzz. Thank God—an excuse to leave for a few minutes.

He stood up and felt dizziness wash over him. Damn. He'd better stop drinking altogether if the little bit he'd had was already beginning to affect him. He excused himself and headed out the door for some quiet and fresh air.

Still feeling a little woozy, he said, "Hello?"

"Blake? It's Grace."

He could barely hear her over the roaring in his ears. "Whass up?"

"We've almost got the Palladian project in the bag, but they have one more important question we have to answer by two o'clock tomorrow. Only you can answer it."

Groggy now, Blake thought that everyone needed

him by two o'clock tomorrow. That's when the wedding was, too. He opened his mouth to ask her what the problem was, but the world tilted and spun as his knees folded and he slumped to the ground in an ungraceful sprawl.

The phone lay only inches from his fingers. He could hear Grace's tinny voice calling his name, but he couldn't muster enough energy to answer her.

One thought came loud and clear through his fogged brain before he passed out. *Damn. They drugged me.*

THE MORNING OF THE wedding, Serena kept Lana busy with preparations. While her mother fluttered around trying to make sure they didn't forget anything for transportation to the falls, Lana's only concern was that she hadn't heard from Blake.

She headed to the bedroom to check for last-minute items and stopped cold. Purple Bunny was back! She snatched him from the bed and hugged him in relief. Everything would be fine now—she wouldn't let her good-luck charm out of her sight until Blake showed up.

The phone rang and she grinned. That must be him now. "Hello?"

"Hello, Lana. It's Grace."

Lana sagged in disappointment. "Oh, hi. What can I do for you?"

"First, I want to say I'm very glad you decided to marry Blake after all, and I hope you'll both be very happy."

"Thanks." *I hope so, too.*

"I, uh, know this is your wedding day, but I really need to speak to Blake. Is he there?"

"No, I haven't seen him all day."

"Damn," Grace said.

"What's wrong?"

"I have to get hold of him by two o'clock to answer a very important bid question."

"Did you try his cell phone?"

"Yes, but he's not answering." She hesitated, then said, "I'm a little concerned. I spoke to him last night, but he sounded funny and we got cut off. I haven't been able to reach him since."

Now Lana was even more uneasy. "Well, he had a bachelor party last night. That may be why he sounded funny. And...maybe he drank a little too much and just hasn't heard the phone yet."

"Maybe," Grace said, but didn't sound as if she believed it. "When you see him, could you ask him to call me if he has a few minutes? It's rather urgent."

"Of course. I know how important this bid is to him."

Lana hung up, really beginning to worry now. Maybe she should send someone to check on him.

Evading her mother's questions, Lana helped her pack the car. When they were almost done, the mayor drove up with Tommie Nell.

"Good morning, Lana," Jimmy said. "We just came by to see if there's anything you need."

She debated whether to admit she hadn't seen or heard from her fiancé, but figured it wouldn't hurt—they'd learn soon enough anyway. "Have you seen Blake?"

"Nope," Jimmy said, "but he got pretty polluted last night. He might be sleeping in."

"That's what I figured. Could you...go by the Sky Hook and check on him?" Jimmy might not want to, but Lana could count on Tommie Nell to ensure he did.

He looked a little reluctant, but Tommie Nell said, "Of course, honey."

"I don't know..." Jimmy said. "He was talking kinda strange last night, like he wasn't planning on showing up at all."

Her heart sank, but Tommie Nell elbowed him in the ribs. "Hush. You're just saying that 'cause you want her to marry Ned."

He shrugged. "If you want to believe that, fine with me." He pointed his cigar at Lana. "But if Warner doesn't show up, you can still marry Ned."

"He's not even in town," Lana protested.

"He will be," Jimmy promised. "He promised me he'd be back in time for the wedding."

Tommie Nell scowled. "Now you stop that, Jimmy Bartlett. You know Lana wants Blake, so you're just gonna have to live with it."

Before the mayor could say anything else, Lana backed away and said, "He'll be there."

I hope.

BLAKE WOKE TO DARKNESS. His head spun in sickening circles, his stomach lurched, his throat was parched and he had one hell of a headache, but he was still alive. He groaned, remembering the men had tricked him into drinking drugged beer. He cursed his own stupidity—he should have known there was more to their plan than just getting him drunk.

Where was he? And what time was it? Had he missed the wedding? He tried to take stock of his surroundings, but couldn't figure out where he was. The floor beneath him was cold and hard, and he could smell mildew and paint, plus other odors he couldn't identify. Was he locked in the back of the town hall?

Well, wherever he was, he had to get out. He blinked and focused on faint lines of light—the outline of a door. He felt the rough, weathered wood of the door and groped for the handle. It was locked.

Beginning to get angry, he ignored the aftereffects of the drug as he fumbled around the interior of his prison for anything that might help. A sweep of his arm sent something crashing to the floor and he leaned down to investigate, smiling when he identified the shape. A hoe.

Grabbing the hoe, he pounded on the door next to the lock, and grimaced in satisfaction when he heard it splinter, revealing a chink of light that illuminated a small patch of the floor.

By now, he'd figured out that he was in a storage shed of some kind, but where? He renewed his attack on the wood until he'd created enough space to get his hand out and feel for the lock. Finally, he was in luck. It was secured only by a metal pin and when he pulled it out, the door swung open.

He blinked in the bright sunlight, recognizing the house across the way. He was on Old Man Feeney's land. No, belay that. It was his father's land now.

How ironic. His father would have approved wholeheartedly if he knew his land had been used to prevent Blake from reaching the wedding.

The wedding! Blake glanced at his watch. One o'clock—and the wedding was at two. Another memory struck him. Grace had spoken to him last night, needing an answer to an urgent question before two. One only *he* could answer.

Well, no problem. He'd do both. He'd call Grace and head for the wedding at the same time, then get some water to soothe his parched throat.

He reached for the cell phone but it was gone. Glancing around frantically, he went back into the shed to see if he'd dropped it there. He didn't find it, but did spot something he hadn't seen before—a canteen sitting in the middle of the floor.

So they hadn't intended for him to die. Mentally thanking the guy who'd left it, Blake quenched his thirst.

One problem down, two to go. His mind worked fast, trying to figure out how he could make it to the wedding *and* call Grace. The falls were at least an hour-long hike up the road, but there was no phone there. The nearest one was at a K-Stop a half hour in the other direction. There was no way he could call Grace *and* make it to the wedding on time.

He stood in indecision for a moment. Grace needed him, and his whole career rode on this bid, not to mention the bet with his father. Could he risk being late to his own wedding?

No, he couldn't. It was bad enough he had to show up without his tux, but to turn up late would be unforgivable—if Lana even waited.

Damn it, he couldn't bear the thought of disappointing her. Grace could handle things without him. She had to. He couldn't let Lana down—she was far more important than his job.

He paused in wonderment, testing that thought in his mind. *Nothing* had ever been more important than his job. Then again, he'd never met anyone like Lana before, either.

Incredulity filled him as he realized the truth. He

loved her. Nothing else could explain why she had suddenly become the most essential element in his life. The thought filled him with joy, and he repeated it to himself in wonder. *I love her.*

Damn. He had to tell her before it was too late. He set off on foot toward the falls, praying he'd make it to the altar on time.

LANA DRESSED for her wedding in the large, striped tent erected for that purpose at the falls. She tried not to fret even though Blake hadn't showed up yet.

But when the tent flap opened and Tommie Nell walked in, Lana squeezed Purple Bunny and asked, "Did you find him?"

Tommie Nell's face creased in apology. "No, honey, we didn't." Pulling Lana aside, she whispered, "He wasn't in his room and Esther said his bed hadn't been slept in. Plus...all his things are gone."

Oh, no. It was worse than she'd thought. He wasn't going to show at all. She covered her mouth with her hand.

Tommie Nell patted her shoulder. "Don't worry, honey, I'm sure he'll be here. He loves you."

No, that was the problem. He didn't.

When Lana didn't—couldn't—say anything, Tommie Nell went on to reassure her. "I'm sure there's a logical explanation."

Seizing on that excuse, Lana said, "Yes, of course. We're staying at my place tonight before we head for Dallas. He probably just packed all his things in the car to save time."

Looking relieved, Tommie Nell said, "That's it. Now don't you worry. Just concentrate on getting pretty."

She hurried out and the others in the tent tried not to let their pity and curiosity show. Of course everyone knew by now that the groom had yet to show up, but Lana still had faith. He'd be there. And if she just kept repeating that to herself, she might even start believing it.

Whatever she did, she had to maintain a calm exterior for her audience. She forced herself to smile reassuringly at Ellie and Kelly, both looking beautiful in pastel bridesmaid dresses.

Serena and Aunt Ona Mae fluttered around to make sure everything was perfect, then Serena led her over to the mirror. Lana's mother clasped her hands to her breast, tears shining in her eyes. "You're so beautiful."

The others echoed her, and Lana stared at her reflection. It was how she'd always pictured herself. She felt a little odd wearing white, but her mother had insisted on the tradition. Lana had given in so she could have her way on other things.

Not wanting to drag a long gown and train across the grass and dirt, she'd chosen a simple A-line dress. Made of shimmery silk, it had puffy sleeves and a sweetheart neckline, and skimmed the top of her knees. It also concealed her pregnancy. She'd bowed to tradition by wearing the smallest possible veil, but secured it on her head with a wreath of her favorite daisies and roses mixed with wildflowers that matched her bouquet.

Now if only the groom would show. Despite herself, Lana felt her lower lip tremble as she clutched the good-luck charm that had promised her happiness. *Come on, you stupid bunny, do your stuff.*

Kelly hugged her, whispering, "He'll be here."

Lana gave her a tremulous smile, hoping she was right.

Auntie Om blanched. "Oh my. You don't think the Bostians got him like they did my Lowell, do you?"

"No, I—"

Suddenly, there was a commotion outside. Ellie's face brightened. "That must be him now."

Still clutching Purple Bunny, Lana rushed to the tent flap and peered out, only to be disappointed. "It's not Blake—it's Ned."

Dressed in a tux with a tall woman at his side, Ned spoke briefly with the mayor, then headed for Lana's tent. The unknown woman followed him, along with the rest of their guests.

When he reached the tent, Lana greeted him in a calm voice. "Hello, Ned."

"I need to speak to you."

She opened the flap wider, and when everyone else would have followed him inside, Ned scowled. "This is private. Everybody out."

Surprisingly, they obeyed him, until only Lana, Ned and the woman were left alone in the tent.

Lana glanced at her, raising an eyebrow.

"This is Fiona," Ned explained. "She's the bus driver who helped me on the wild-goose chase Jimmy sent me on."

"What wild-goose chase?"

"Never mind—I'll explain later. Fiona got me back here on time for the wedding so I figure she deserves to stay."

Lana shrugged, not caring if she stayed or not, though the unhappy look on Fiona's face made Lana wonder why she wanted to.

Ned took a deep breath, then spoke. "I'm here as promised, and I'll still marry you."

His demeanor was more that of a man sentenced to life imprisonment than one who was about to celebrate his nuptials. He slanted an apologetic look at Fiona, who appeared even more unhappy. The two exchanged a fervent glance.

Suddenly Lana realized what it signified—they were in love with each other. But Ned's misplaced loyalty required him to honor his promise to Lana.

"That's not necessary. I chose Blake."

Fiona turned an expectant face to Ned, but his expression hardened. "I know, but I also know he's not here and the ceremony is scheduled to start in five minutes."

Five minutes! Where was he? "He'll be here," she said with a confidence she didn't feel.

"But—"

Cheers and groans from outside cut off whatever Ned was about to say. Lana rushed to the tent flap. Could it be Blake?

She couldn't see for all the people in the way until they gasped and the crowd parted. Blake stood in the center, his fists cocked as he glared down at Ralph. The poor man lay on the ground, holding his jaw and staring up at Blake with a look of horror.

Blake was angry, disheveled and dirty, but she didn't care. He looked wonderful.

Raising his fists again, Blake glared around at the crowd. "Anyone else want to try and keep me from Lana?"

He wanted her! Not caring about tradition or superstitious nonsense, Lana dropped Purple Bunny and burst through the tent opening to fly across the grass.

Throwing her arms about his neck, she said, "I was so worried. What happened to you?"

He gently held her away from his body. "I don't want to get your dress dirty." Then, glaring at the mayor, he said, "I almost didn't make it. Someone drugged my beer at the party last night and dumped me in Old Man Feeney's shed. Lucky for me I didn't drink as much as they thought or I'd still be there."

The crowd murmured and Ralph scrambled to his feet, backing away from Blake's murderous expression.

Blake stared down at Lana, still holding her at arm's length. "But I'm here now and—" He broke off, his face tightening as his gaze fixed on something behind her.

She glanced over her shoulder. Ned was right behind her, Fiona at his side.

Blake faced Lana, looking fierce. "I know I'm late and I don't deserve you, but please give me another chance."

Seeing how he could misconstrue Ned's presence, she said, "But—"

"No, please hear me out." Blake dropped to one knee in front of the startled townspeople and clasped Lana's hand, looking up at her with an earnest expression. "I had a lot of time to think this morning, and when I thought I would lose you, I suddenly realized I love you with all my heart. I don't want to live without you. Please, will you marry me?"

Joy filled her heart, making her unable to speak for a moment. He loved her! Her eyes filled with tears, and she managed to choke out, "Yes."

An expression of delight spread across his face, and Blake leapt to his feet to kiss her.

"Wait," Jimmy bellowed. "You can't do that. You have to marry Ned."

Before Lana or Blake could say anything, Ned said, "No, she doesn't."

The mayor scowled and pointed his cigar at Ned. "You keep out of this—"

"No, I won't," Ned said. "I only offered to take Blake's place to fulfill my promise. She doesn't have to marry me, because..." He drew the bus driver forward. "I'm marrying Fiona."

Jimmy spluttered. "But—"

"Today," Ned interjected. "That is, if Blake and Lana don't mind sharing their wedding ceremony."

They assured him they didn't, and the mayor's face cleared. "Today? Well, that's all right then." With a smug glance, he grinned at Tommie Nell. "Looks like the legend will be satisfied after all."

Ignoring the muttering of the crowd, Blake turned to Lana. "I need a little time to get cleaned up. I'm sorry I don't have my tux here, but do you mind if I marry you in this?" He glanced down at his jeans and dirt-streaked shirt.

"I don't care," Lana said. "The important thing is that you're here."

The mayor cleared his throat and approached them, saying, "Well, that, uh, won't be necessary. I have your things in my trunk, for...safekeeping, you understand."

Blake raised an eyebrow. "Safekeeping?" He laughed. "Right now, I don't care. I'm just glad you have them."

He grinned down at Lana. "Give me a few minutes to change and clean up?"

"Of course."

"Great." He gave her a swift kiss. "See you at the altar."

While he dressed, Lana had one last thing to do. She hurried back to the tent and picked up Purple Bunny. "Thanks," she whispered in his ear. "I should have never doubted you."

Wanting to spread the wealth now that she'd found the happiness the note had promised, Lana decided to pass him on to Ellie. Kelly was already engaged, though Lana didn't care much for her fiancé, so Ellie needed someone, too.

Quickly Lana scribbled a note and stuffed it in his pouch. Perfect timing—Ellie and Kelly walked in just as she zipped him up. "What are you doing?" Kelly asked.

Lana thrust the stuffed animal into Ellie's arms. "I'm passing Purple Bunny to Ellie. This is definitely a special occasion and it's her turn to have him."

Ellie gave the rabbit a doubtful glance. "Gee, thanks, but I think I'll leave him here until the wedding is over." She set him down and cocked her head at the sound of music. "There's our cue." She grinned. "Good luck, Lana."

"Yeah," Kelly said, hugging her. "You deserve the best."

The ceremony proceeded without a hitch. Lost in a happy haze, Lana felt as if it were something out of a dream. Her wedding was exactly how she'd always pictured it—facing the glorious beauty of the falls with her best friends standing by her, the townspeople supporting her at her back and a loving husband at her side.

When it was over and her new husband claimed her with a heart-stopping kiss, Lana's joy was complete. Even the thought of moving to Dallas didn't daunt her. She could withstand anything, knowing Blake loved her.

Happier than she'd ever been in her life, Lana headed toward the picnic pavilion where she and Blake formed a reception line along with the other couple to receive their guests. Blake seemed surprised at the abundant good wishes people expressed to him, but she wasn't. She knew her neighbors couldn't fail to appreciate his wonderful qualities, once they'd gotten past that silly legend.

The mayor approached Blake. "Say, the boys and I have something to ask you—"

Jimmy was interrupted by a buzzing sound coming from his pocket. Looking sheepish, he pulled out Blake's cell phone and handed it to him. "I, uh, was keeping this for you, too."

Blake raised an eyebrow. "I wish I'd known you had that. I could have called Grace."

Lana gasped. "I forgot—she had an urgent question. You mean you haven't talked to her yet?"

He shrugged. "No, it was either find a phone or make it here on time."

And he'd chosen *her*. Despite the feeling of satisfaction that gave her, Lana said, "But the company, your father..."

"This may be him. Hold on." He answered the phone, then covered the mouthpiece. "It's Grace. Would you mind if I excuse myself for a few minutes while I find out what happened?"

"Of course not." She just hoped he hadn't lost everything he cared about to be with her.

Blake secluded himself in a tent and Lana continued greeting her guests, assuring them he would be back soon. Fifteen minutes later, he returned.

Unable to tell what had happened from his deadpan expression, she asked, "How'd it go?"

His face spread into a grin. "Grace didn't need me after all. She convinced them the question was irrelevant and we were the best company for the job. They agreed and promised to award it to us tomorrow."

"That's wonderful. So now you have full control of Warner Construction?"

"Not quite."

Puzzled that he didn't seem upset, she asked, "What do you mean?"

He leaned down and whispered, "I traded control of the company for your wedding present."

No present was worth him losing his dream. "But—"

"Don't you want to know what it is?"

He seemed so pleased with himself that she swallowed her anxiety and said, "Of course."

"It's...the Bachelor Falls Resort."

Surprise widened her eyes. "You mean..."

"Yes. Old Man Feeney's land now belongs to me—lock, stock, and barrel."

"Oh, Blake," she whispered in pleased disbelief. "You did it. You saved the town. But...what about you? That company was everything to you, and you sacrificed it all for us."

He kissed her nose. "Not really. It's everything to my father, not to me. I traded because he agreed to give me the land and make Grace the CEO of Warner Construction."

"Is that what Grace wants?"

"Yes. She was ecstatic, and my father was satisfied, too."

Satisfied? "But, have your parents reconciled to our marriage?" She doubted it—they hadn't even bothered to show up for their son's wedding.

"Not yet," Blake said. "But don't worry, they'll come around. I'm their only son, and you're carrying their only grandchild. When my mother heard that, she changed her tune."

For his sake, Lana hoped he was right. "Well, now that you're out of a job, what do you plan to do?"

Looking sheepish, he said, "Well, I kind of like it here. Since I never had anything to spend it on, I have some money saved up, enough to live on for a while. I thought we could build a house on that land, raise some kids, maybe do some fishing...?"

Lana couldn't believe it. He was giving her everything she'd ever wanted. "Are you sure this is what *you* want?"

"I'm sure. I've never been happier or more fulfilled than I am here—even if your neighbors do drive us nuts." He grinned. "Now all I need to do is find something to do. Maybe I could hire out as a handyman."

The mayor tapped Blake on the shoulder, a bunch of his henchmen behind him. He gestured at his cronies with his cigar. "We wanted to apologize for any problems we might have caused you." He thrust his chin out. "But, dang it, we couldn't let you mess up the legend."

Jimmy clammed up. Apparently that was as much of an apology as he was willing to give.

Blake kept him hanging for a moment or two while

he considered their apology. "I understand. And right now, I don't think I could be mad at anybody."

"Yeah. Everything worked out for the best." Looking relieved, Jimmy added, "I couldn't help but overhear. Did you say you were staying in Bachelor Falls?"

"Yes."

"Then me and the boys would like you to consider a little proposition."

"What kind of proposition?" Blake asked.

"Well, we could use a man with your expertise. You told us yourself we need a town manager, and we figured you're the best man for the job. How about it? It don't pay much, but we'd be real obliged."

It was perfect for him. Silently Lana urged him to take it.

Blake grinned. "I'd be glad to be your new town manager…after the honeymoon, of course."

"Of course, of course," the mayor said. "We'll discuss your salary and duties when you get back. Have a nice trip." Having said his piece, he hustled his "boys" out of the way.

"Let's get out of here," Lana whispered. She wanted to be alone with Blake.

"Good idea. But don't we have some things to do first?"

"Yes, but it won't take long. They'll be happy enough to have Ned and Fiona here."

They cut the cake, managing not to smash it on each other's faces, then signed the license, did the obligatory garter and bouquet toss and exited in a shower of birdseed as they raced toward the waiting limo.

They dashed into the back seat, laughing, and shut

the door. Blake kissed her. "Did you see the expression on Jimmy's face when I threw the garter right into his hands?"

"Yeah—it was almost as funny as the horror on Ellie's when I hit her square in the chest with the bouquet."

They both chuckled and their driver, Ralph, turned around, sporting one heck of a shiner. "Where'll it be, folks?"

Blake smiled down at her. "So, Mrs. Warner, now that we have time for a honeymoon, where would you like to go? Anywhere you want—London, Paris, Rome, you name it."

She shrugged. "I just want to be with you. Would you mind if we went to the cabin? It's where my parents spent their honeymoon."

He grinned. "Perfect." Raising his voice, he told Ralph, "Drive us to Lana's and we'll take it from there."

As Ralph started the car, they waved goodbye to their well-wishers, and Lana turned to Blake. Grinning, she huffed on his lapel and rubbed the spot with her knuckles.

"What's that for?"

"Oh, nothing. I thought there was a smudge there, but I was wrong. My white knight's armor is still bright, shiny and totally unblemished."

Epilogue

Bachelor Falls Gazette
Evening Edition
August 13, 1998

New Resident Arrives!

Early this morning, a new resident arrived in Bachelor Falls, kicking and screaming. Matthew Edward, weighing in at eight pounds three ounces, was born to Blake and Lana Warner at the Bachelor Falls clinic. His mother and father are both doing fine, though it was questionable for a while if Daddy would survive the experience.

Immediately after delivery, Matthew was greeted by his maternal grandmother, Serena Talbot, who gifted him on the spot with a playpen. Sources close to the family report that it's twice as large as the one Melva Whiffington gave her daughter! His doting paternal grandparents presented their daughter-in-law with a diamond bracelet, giving the baby a large trust fund along with dozens of toys. This lucky little boy has so many gifts already, he'll need that brand-new house his daddy built to hold them all!

Little Matthew will be at home in a few days and his proud parents invite everyone to drop by and meet the youngest resident of Bachelor Falls.

Friends of the family will be relieved to hear that Ona Mae Hunyacre, our local expert on extraterrestrials, examined the baby and declared him to be totally alien-free.

The spring 1998 forecast calls for...

Showers

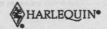

April 1998: **HERE COMES THE...BABY**
Pam McCutcheon
A front of morning sickness sets in with
temperatures rising at the onset of a sexy secret
dad. Highs: Too hot!

May 1998: **A BACHELOR FALLS**
   Karen Toller Whittenburg
Heavy gusts of romance continue as a warming
trend turns friends to lovers just in time for one
friend's wedding...to someone else!

June 1998: **BRIDE TO BE...OR NOT
   TO BE?** Debbi Rawlins
Expect a heat wave as the handsome hunk
building a bride's dream house sends soaring
temperatures through her fantasies.

Available wherever Harlequin books are sold.

HARLEQUIN®

Take 4 bestselling love stories FREE

Plus get a FREE surprise gift!

Special Limited-time Offer

Mail to Harlequin Reader Service®

3010 Walden Avenue
P.O. Box 1867
Buffalo, N.Y. 14240-1867

YES! Please send me 4 free Harlequin American Romance® novels and my free surprise gift. Then send me 4 brand-new novels every month, which I will receive months before they appear in bookstores. Bill me at the low price of $3.34 each plus 25¢ delivery and applicable sales tax, if any.* That's the complete price and a savings of over 10% off the cover prices—quite a bargain! I understand that accepting the books and gift places me under no obligation ever to buy any books. I can always return a shipment and cancel at any time. Even if I never buy another book from Harlequin, the 4 free books and the surprise gift are mine to keep forever.

154 HEN CE7C

Name _____ (PLEASE PRINT)

Address _____ Apt. No. _____

City _____ State _____ Zip _____

This offer is limited to one order per household and not valid to present Harlequin American Romance® subscribers. *Terms and prices are subject to change without notice. Sales tax applicable in N.Y.

UAM-696   ©1990 Harlequin Enterprises Limited

Presents
Extravaganza

25 YEARS!

It's our birthday and we're celebrating....

Twenty-five years of romance fiction
featuring men of the world and captivating women—
Seduction and passion guaranteed!

Not only are we promising you three months of terrific
books, authors and romance, but as an added **bonus**
with the retail purchase of two Presents® titles,
you can receive a special one-of-a-kind keepsake.
It's our gift to you!

Look in the back pages of any Harlequin Presents® title,
from May to July 1998, for more details.

Available wherever Harlequin books are sold.

◆ HARLEQUIN®

Catch more great

HARLEQUIN™ Movies

featured on the movie channel ⓣⓜⓒ

Premiering April 11th
Hard to Forget
based on the novel by bestselling
Harlequin Superromance® author
Evelyn A. Crowe

Don't miss next month's movie!
Premiering May 9th
The Awakening
starring Cynthia Geary and David Beecroft
based on the novel by Patricia Coughlin

If you are not currently a subscriber to
The Movie Channel, simply call your
local cable or satellite provider for more
details. Call today, and don't miss out
on the romance!

100% pure movies.
100% pure fun.

HARLEQUIN™
Makes any time special ™

Act now
to receive these favorite
By Request® collections!

#20114	LEGENDARY LOVERS by Debbie Macomber	$5.50 U.S. ☐ $5.99 CAN.☐	
#20116	SURRENDER! by Kathleen Eagle	$5.50 U.S. ☐ $5.99 CAN.☐	
#20129	ROYAL WEDDINGS	$5.99 U.S. ☐ $6.99 CAN.☐	
#20130	HOME FOR CHRISTMAS	$5.99 U.S. ☐ $6.99 CAN.☐	
#20133	YOURS, MINE & OURS	$5.99 U.S. ☐ $6.99 CAN.☐	
#20135	A MATCH FOR MOM	$5.99 U.S. ☐ $6.99 CAN.☐	

(quantities may be limited on some titles)

TOTAL AMOUNT	$
POSTAGE & HANDLING	$
($1.00 for one book, 50¢ for each additional)	
APPLICABLE TAXES*	$ _____
TOTAL PAYABLE	$ _____

(check or money order—please do not send cash)

To order, complete this form and send it, along with a check or money order for the total above, payable to By Request, to: **In the U.S.:** 3010 Walden Avenue, P.O. Box 9047, Buffalo, NY 14269-9047; **In Canada:** P.O. Box 613, Fort Erie, Ontario, L2A 5X3.

Name: _____

Address: _____ City: _____

State/Prov.: _____ Zip/Postal Code: _____

Account Number: _____

*New York residents remit applicable sales taxes.
Canadian residents remit applicable GST and provincial taxes.   075 CSAS

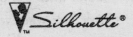

Look us up on-line at: http://www.romance.net   PBRBL1